XTREMIS

JOSE DEGRACIA

XTREMIS

Copyright © 2021 Jose DeGracia

Cover Illustration by Kory Cromie

Editing by Jessica Hatch, Hatch Editorial Services

Cover and Interior Layout by Becky's Graphic Design®, LLC

ISBN: 978-1-7373383-0-7 (Hardcover)
ISBN: 978-1-7373383-1-4 (eBook)

Printed in United States of America

First Edition

For Mikey,

For Martin,

For Luna,

For Becca

Thank you for believing in me.

THE FRACTURE

Sometime soon...

KCL Campground – Santa Margarita, California

Hector hated going camping. His stepfather insisted they go as a family at least twice a year, but at least during the winter they could do cool stuff, like sled in the mountains. The heat was what bothered him. It was always too hot to sleep, not to mention having to share a car with his parents. He never understood white people's obsession with living like cavemen. Cavemen that still needed air mattresses in their neon yellow tents. He knew that David was trying his best to be a good father, but no one was really going to compare to Dad. Dad let them sleep inside, where there was AC and internet. The Angels were playing tonight, too. Hector just wanted to go home.

"Hector!" his mom yelled.

He snapped out of his train of thought. "Whaat?!" he whined back.

"Don't 'What?' me. It's time to eat. Put the video games down and let's go," his mother, Marlene, responded.

Hector put away his portable game console. He was so close to finishing. 'Why can't she just let me do my thing?' he thought. He never got any real time to himself. He doubted anybody else wanted to be around a fourteen-year-old either, so why did they bug him so much?

"What are we eating?" he asked, hoping David hadn't killed

anything. The animals had it bad enough out here with nothing around to eat, he thought. They didn't need David trying to kill them.

"David brought steaks in the cooler," his mom said. "He's over by the grill there. Go talk to him, he knows about all this stuff. It's gorgeous out here, and you're staring at the ground."

"But I—"

"But nothing, *mijo*. He tries his best for all of us, and you should get to know him better." Hector kicked a rock. "Okay," he said. "I'll give it a shot."

Hector kept his eyes on the ground as he walked towards the grilling area. It wasn't hard to find in the remote campsite. In fact, there was barely an outhouse there. Rangers would come twice a day to clean and refill it, but otherwise civilization was whatever campers brought with them.

"Who even chooses to come out here?" Hector said to himself. He dragged his way to where David was cooking at and tapped his shoulder.

"Oh hey, buddy. You hungry?" David smiled. "Yeah... I didn't know you brought steaks."

"Well, there's not much fishing to do out here in the desert!" David joked.

Hector didn't laugh. He looked at him, then back at his mother, who was preparing some food on the picnic table. The sunset cast a warm blanket across the entirety of the campsite.

"Why did we come all the way out here?"

David cleared his throat. "You know, the stars are about to come out. You could probably count them all if you really tried out here." He gestured with his spatula to the sky.

"You didn't answer the question," Hector said. "I know you want us to be one big family and all, but why can't we do it, I dunno, literally anywhere else? There's nowhere to even plug in my chargers, and everything is dying."

David frowned. He was really trying to get through to this kid. His new wife was just happy to have a father figure in her son's life, but Hector couldn't get on the same wavelength. " I feel like you're missing the point here." He handed Hector the tray of mid-rare steaks. "Let's continue this while we eat."

The family sat down to eat at the picnic table. Everyone took turns selecting a steak and various side items to pair with it. As they munched, David spoke up again. "You wanna know why I brought you guys out here?" Hector glanced at his mom. She raised her eyebrows.

"Yeah." Hector swallowed a bite. "Why?"

"Well, I just want you guys to get a real appreciation for Mother Nature. We've been to Yellowstone, we've been to the mountains, but that's not everything the planet has to offer us. There's beauty out here, too."

"But there's nothing out here," Hector said. "It's all dead or dry. I can smell Los Angeles from here. Nothing is going to grow."

David shook his head as though his stepson wasn't getting it. "I'm not talking about plants and trees. I'm talking about another side of nature. The scary side. The side that thrives in places like this. The part of nature that says, 'I can take whatever you throw at me.' The side that, no matter what we do as people, we can't affect. In fact, over that ridge, there is a cliff that overlooks the valley. Underground is the epicenter of the San Andreas Fault. So every little earthquake you or anyone else in this country has experienced resonated from right over there."

Hector looked over to where David was pointing. He hadn't realized that it had gotten dark while they were eating. A trail from the edge of the campground led to some rocks that obscured the cliff.

"In the morning, we're taking a hike down the trail and getting a good look at the valley as soon as the sun peeks over the horizon."

"Wait, the morning?" Hector asked in horror. "That means—"

"Yup." David nodded. "We're waking up before dawn. So get your plates cleaned up because we're going to bed."

Hector groaned. Reluctantly, he got himself cleaned up and ready for bed. He checked his phone one more time outside of the tent. No signal, no messages. Hector sighed as he sat on the bench near the tent. He looked up at the stars, though. Even he had to admit he was taken aback by how pretty it looked.

"I told you you could count them all."

David had exited the outhouse in his pajamas and made his way over to Hector. He sat down next to him and took in the view as well.

"David?"

"Yeah, buddy?"

"I still don't get it. Why do you insist on making us go on these trips?"

David pondered for a moment while he looked at the cosmos. "Take a look at any star up there. Pick just one to concentrate on."

Hector did. "Okay."

"Now think about the hypothetical idea that, maybe, it's a star just like our sun. Think about the possibility that there happens to be a planet just like ours orbiting it, with all the sustainability and room and air and everything else needed for life to grow on it."

"Okay."

"Now think about the hypothetical idea that we can't stay here on our planet anymore. The skies are smoggy, the water's brown, and the ozone is depleting more and more."

"So let's go to that other planet, hypothetically," Hector suggested.

"Sure, hypothetically let's do that. But what if all that stuff I said about the planet was real? And we had no way of leaving. What then?"

"We..." Hector had to think for a moment. "Is that true?"

"It's not false," David replied. "With everything going on in the world just spiraling out of control, the best thing we can do is try to experience what's left of nature before it's all gone. Or before she fights back."

Hector sat there, thinking about all the times he had endured these trips. They were all different. The mountains during the winter, camping at Yellowstone, out here in the desert, even when they visited that farm out in Bakersfield, they all made at least a bit more sense now.

"On that note, I'm going to bed. Sorry to give you all that to process." David made his way back towards the tent.

"David?" Hector called after him. "Yeah, bud?"

"I'm... sorry for being a downer all the time."

He could barely see the shadow of David's grin. "Oh. No worries, man. I know you've got stuff on your mind all the time."

"Well, thanks. I used to think that you were... I dunno. Kinda lame. But I know you love Mom, and that's the big picture here. I just want to say, thanks for everything."

David smiled at him. "Aw. Thanks, kid. Try to get some sleep tonight, okay? We've got an early—"

A thunderous explosion threw them to the ground.

"What the hell was that?!" Hector shouted. He looked over at the tent. His mother was fighting her way out of the collapsed shelter.

"David?! Hector?!" his mother yelled. "What's going on?"

The earth shook beneath them as the family scrambled to huddle together. Ungodly sounds howled with rage in the fault below them. The cliffside gave way to the valley, exposing them to what had transpired.

"Oh my god." David could barely get the words out as he looked out over the valley. The fault had opened up, creating a massive sieve into the ground. He managed to compose himself for a moment. "Is everybody okay?"

"What the hell?" Hector couldn't help saying. All of those nice things David had said about nature could go screw themselves. "Of course we're not okay!"

"Hector, get in the truck!" His mom ran to the vehicle while covering her ears. The howls were getting louder.

"Yeah, one sec!" Hector saw David transfixed at the edge of the new cliff formation. He ran over and grabbed him. "David, we gotta go man!" He stopped in his tracks when he noticed a glow on David's face. It was warm and orange as if the sun had returned. David hadn't blinked. Hector looked down at the new canyon. His jaw dropped while he tried to process what he was looking at. An unholy screech shook them both out of their stupor. Their eyes followed something up into the sky. It burned brightly, as beautiful as it was terrifying. It banked in the sky and glided towards them.

"RUN!" David yelled.

Hector was frozen in his tracks, watching the horror in the sky, when David shook him back into the moment. The men took off running to the truck. The family piled in and strapped on their seatbelts as David peeled onto the dirt road in front of them. Hector tried to console his mother, who was crying uncontrollably in the back seat, while David was trying his best not to panic while driving in the getaway vehicle.

In the rearview mirror David could see the glow from the new canyon get brighter. It illuminated the dark dirt road the lonely vehicle traveled.

"What was that?!" Marlene screamed. "I've never heard anything like that."

"I... I don't know." David shuddered. "I've... I've never—"

"Look!" Hector pointed out the window. Darkness covered the valley, and the road began to crack and crumble. The vehicle swerved as David tried to keep them on solid ground. The light in the sky followed them, screeching as it came. Hector looked out to see the first light source separate into another one.

"Something just dripped out of that thing!" he reported. "What? What are you talking about!?" David yelled.

A bright light shot past the car on the road. It glanced the front driver's side and forced him to swerve to the side of the highway. Everything was silent for a moment. The family was hyperventilating, trying to comprehend what was happening. Everybody seemed to be okay, panic notwithstanding.

"Davi—"

"Shh!" The car stood alone on the dirt road. The light in the sky was gone. The light that shot past was nowhere to be seen. The howling had subsided. They were alone.

"We have to go, David," Hector managed to pipe up.

"You're right." David started to crank the car back up. Nothing. He tried the starter again, nothing was working. He slammed on the steering wheel. The now familiar orange glow from the canyon was growing. Hector saw the source getting closer to the vehicle.

"Is that, is that lava?" Hector asked no one. The red-hot goop was slowly making its way towards the car, igniting fences, killing wildlife, and burning a swath through the night.

David kept trying to crank the damaged vehicle up again. Still nothing. Marlene screamed, "We have to get out of here, we have to–"

She was interrupted by a force slamming into the truck. A brightly glowing beast clawed at its side, howling and slashing, tearing bit by bit into the metal doors. The family scrambled to the opposite side of the vehicle only to be rocked by a second jolt. Another glowing monster was trying to get at them from that side, screeching and howling all the same. David slammed on the dashboard, trying to get the car to start. He wrenched on the keys one more time.

The engine sputtered to life, and David slammed on the gas. The car managed to get about a hundred feet away from the two glowing beasts before the engine finally sputtered to a halt and.

"Oh god!" Marlene cried.

"It's okay, they're not moving! They're just sitting there," Hector observed from the back seat. The animals watched the now immobile vehicle, almost curiously. They gnawed on the pieces of metal they had ripped from the car. "What are they?"

David had no answer. He was resolved to get everyone out of there safe. "Wait here."

"What? No!" Hector and his mother pleaded for David to stay, but he was already kicking his door open.

The animals didn't move towards him. They were motionless, staring up into the sky. David crept toward the hood of the car. The damage was extensive, as steam and smoke billowed out of the engine block. David halted in his tracks when he realized the glow around him wasn't from the beasts or the lava flow, but from above him.

Inside the car, Hector and his mother kept their eyes on the monsters behind them. After a moment, Marlene noticed David hadn't come back yet.

"D-D-D-D-David?" she shook. He should have been done by now. The car was sweltering at this point, as if the planet was pulling itself closer to the sun. The windows were destroyed, and the lava was getting closer. "Hector, we have to get out of here. David is—"

David's body fell, hitting the windshield, shattering it and rolling off, closing the hood in the process. In front of the vehicle was a winged, glowing beast. It screeched so loudly as blood dripped from its beak that Marlene and Hector could barely protect their ears. Hector saw that the lava had almost reached the beasts behind them.

Amidst the commotion, he didn't notice that more animals had shown up, dozens, maybe more.

The lava, they're walking in it!

The winged beast at the front of the car started chewing on David's corpse. Hector and his mother held each other, crying and waiting for something to happen.

"I love you, Mom!"

"I love you, too!"

When the beasts charged, the car was enveloped by glowing light. They tore the vehicle and those inside to shreds.

THORNTON

20 Years Later...

Resistance Forward Operating Base, somewhere in Louisiana

Dr. Craig Thornton's trench coat swept behind him as he walked down the corridor to the base's helipad. He pushed his glasses up the bridge of his nose and, despite the way they fogged when he walked out onto the swampy bayou, he kept his attention solely on the datapad in front of him.

He muttered to himself, "Bringing me out to the middle of the bloody swamp..." while two armored soldiers opened up the passageway. No matter how long he stayed in this godforsaken country, so far from the bustle of London even in the state it was in, he would never get used to it. The bulkhead gave way to the helipad high atop the platform at the north tower of the base. Thornton climbed into the transport helicopter, strapped himself in, and signaled the pilot to take off. The pilot gave a thumbs-up to the crewman and pulled the helicopter into the air. Thornton was so absorbed in the information at his fingertips he didn't even realize he wasn't alone in the passenger area.

"Craig, you've got to realize that eventually you're going to walk right into a Demon," said a suited man. Thornton recognized him just by hearing his voice.

"Cresher, you know that name is absurd. 'Demon' implies that the life-forms came from hell itself, which opens up a realm of possibilities that would envelop the planet faster than they have," he replied, still looking at his datapad.

"Who's to say that they aren't? If you were to ask any human what a Demon looks like, I'm pretty sure that's exactly what they would describe." Cresher quipped as he raised an eyebrow. His white hair was slicked back with product. His tailored suit fitted to his exact measurements with a subtle yet bright red, white, and blue, American flag pinned to his lapel. The picture of luxury in a time of societal survival. To him, it never really mattered what they looked like, all that mattered was the contract he got to run this program and all the zeros on the bottom line.

"They're not demons," Thornton countered. "If they're demons as people like to say, then that implies the devil himself is here waging a holy war. There are no angels, and there is no God smiting the devil and his armies here. No God, no devil, no army from heaven or hell. It's just us."

"That's incredibly bleak," Cresher replied, frowning.

"It's not so bad. We're still here fighting back. If the devil and God were really fighting over us, we wouldn't last this long," Thornton said with a grin.

Cresher folded his arms. "God, I wish I were as optimistic as you. Unfortunately, though, that's not my job. My job is to ensure the future of the human race. It's why I'm here to pick you up. It's why we're leaving together to get the next one. We can rendezvous with the rest of this project there. Do you have your equipment with you?"

"Always." Thornton rubbed his weaponized wrist gauntlets. "They're not the best when dealing with the beasts, but they'll do in a pinch."

"Good. Lucky for you, you won't be spending too much time on the front line. You're here more for your brain than anything else. Tactics, R&D, I got a Sudoku puzzle that's been pissing me off, and of course, weapons engineering." Cresher extended his hand, offering a friendly shake.

Thornton looked at it for a moment, and then studied Cresher. His glasses brought up information from universal databases on his new liaison.

NAME: PETER CRESHER

Age: 52

Known Associations: U.S. Government, FBI, CIA

Occupation: Resistance Liaison To The United States

Heart Rate: Normal

"I'm in." Thornton took the handshake. Cresher smiled and brushed back his hair. Maybe in this war, Thornton thought, it was finally the right time for the humans to come together to fight back.

They weren't going to have much choice soon anyway. "Where are we headed?" Thornton asked as he sat down.

"Here, let me send it to you." Cresher tapped his own datapad's screen and sent the pertinent info over to Thornton's.

The British import pushed up his glasses as he downloaded the message. He took a close look at the numbers and information on his screen.

"What? We're going to Texas for this? You can't be serious."

"Incredibly serious."

"H-How? I thought Arthur Morris was among those who died in the first wave."

"They found his body and salvaged it," Cresher said. "Put it into this program that the government has violently shoved into overdrive for the last twenty years. He was a good candidate. After all, before all this, he was a top-notch actor and martial artist."

"What is it with you Americans and your action movies? You want to put whatever this is at the front and center of this project?" Thornton asked.

"Let me counter your question with another question. Why would the United States bankroll this entire resistance pushback operation without any American augmented individuals on this team?"

Thornton parsed over a few comebacks but ended up surrendering, at least for the moment. "Fair enough, but since you want me to be a player coach for this outfit, I get final approval on the squad." He gestured to Cresher's datapad. "If you want to put this thing on the point, I'll need to make sure it's not a liability."

"Deal. Less work for me." Cresher sat back in his seat, pulled out a blindfold from his briefcase, put it on, and proceeded to take a nap.

Thornton, meanwhile, scanned through the new information on his datapad.

Does he even know yet?

Thornton pondered the days to come and the lives they could save if this final initiative worked. Mankind was on its last legs. The Barrier was only going to hold out for so long. Thornton knew that the minds and bodies of men could only do so much against the forces of Mother Nature herself. The monstrosities that had come and the ones yet to arrive were all constant reminders that man was insignificant in the eyes of the universe. Thornton felt tired. He wondered how people like Cresher could fall asleep at a moment's notice in a helicopter during a storm.

The helicopter flew into the darkening clouds, westbound for their next location.

CHAPTER 2

THE PROGRAM

The helicopter carrying Cresher and Thornton landed on the helipad of what Thornton assumed used to be the stadium the Dallas Cowboys played in. The sports arena had been repurposed almost immediately after the Fracture had occurred. As they exited the chopper, the two were met by a bespectacled doctor in a lab coat.

"Dr. Simmons!" Cresher exclaimed. "I'm excited to see what you have prepared for us today."

Dr. Simmons was surprised by the weaponized hand he grasped as he shook Thornton's hand. He marveled at the gear. "You must be Dr. Craig Thornton. I've heard about your research on your equipment here. Very interesting stuff. I'm going to want to see a demonstration later."

Thornton flinched. "Erm. Only if necessary, I don't get the chance to maintain it very much.

In fact, I'd love to check out your facilities and do some repairs."

"Absolutely. The Xtremis Project welcomes you to the family. What's ours is yours to use. We're very excited to launch, forgive us if we're buzzing." The doctor waved for them to follow him inside.

Thornton and Cresher glanced at each other. Cresher flashed a grin and followed the energetic man inside. Thornton looked around the landing zone. There was much less security than he had anticipated, which was certainly a reason for concern.

"Dr. Simmons, what exactly is this facility used for?" he asked.

"I assume you've been briefed by our friend, Mr. Cresher, here?" the doctor replied.

"Yes, but I want to hear it from you. What's going on here?" Thornton adjusted his gauntlets as the party was led deeper into the facility. The elevator was very obviously added post-Fracture. It seemed pieced together with scraps and felt very out of place. The shaft looked like it was dug directly into the ground.

Dr. Simmons opened the gate to the elevator, and the three men piled in. "I will happily show you once we get in the lab. We're going to activate him for the first time today."

"Tell me more about this Xtremis program," Thornton pressed. Dr. Simmons pushed the button designated "Lab" in what looked like permanent marker on some electrical tape. "From what I'm getting, you rebuilt this guy, this Arthur Morris, and made him a killing machine."

"Well, it just sounds sinister if you say it like that," Dr. Simmons said innocently. "No, there is much more to it than that. Arthur is the culmination of decades of research and experimentation."

The elevator creaked to a halt, and they made their way down the corridor. Simmons continued as they walked. "If our calculations are correct, he will have been, in his mind, only asleep for a moment. It will be as if he jumped through time twenty years into his future." He gave a nervous grin. "His mind may not survive the experience. "

"Hold on, what the fuck?" Cresher exploded. "Simmons. We had a deal. The fate of the planet lies with this program, and you don't know if he's going to make it?" Thornton was surprised at how fast his teammate had dropped his carefree demeanor. "If this doesn't work, I swear to Christ I will—"

"You also accelerated our timetable by years," Simmons responded, refusing to back down. "This is the best shot we have. He's the only one whose brain we've managed to keep alive for this long."

Cresher could barely contain his rage. Thornton observed that his fist was balled up and shaking behind his back. He seemed to freeze for a moment, then to force his anger back down where it had come from.

"Well then, doctor," he said, "I guess we know what happens if this doesn't work. The government will make sure your corpse gets deposited directly into The Fracture itself, along with the tactical nuke they so desperately want to drop." Cresher's eyes narrowed as he brushed his hair back. It seemed as if doing so brought him back down to earth. Thornton couldn't help but smile; Cresher had always seemed unfazed by the apocalypse going on around him. It was nice to see that he did, in fact, have a tipping point.

Dr. Simmons merely smirked at Cresher's remarks. "Follow me then, gentlemen." He led them to another doorway, this one was much more elaborate and secure than Thornton had seen from the rest of the facility. Simmons put his hand on the biometric scanner, which beeped and flashed green before opening up to a simple keypad. He went to put in his number but stopped for a moment. He looked at Cresher and Thornton. They both looked away while he typed in his passcode and unlocked the secure door. Once they stepped through, the door hissed shut behind them.

Inside was a plethora of scientists, doctors, lab technicians, and armed security guards. All were furiously finishing last-minute details in preparation for the big moment.

"So this is where all the money went. You sure being this far underground is a good idea? What with the enemy being... underground and all?" Thornton asked aloud.

"We have multiple facilities," Simmons responded. "Once there weren't any sports being played, there was a lot of extra real estate that wasn't being used. It's another reason the program took so long. Once a facility was compromised in any way, we had to pick up and move. All of those years of working on the run will be worth it in less than thirty minutes."

"What the hell?" Cresher finally got a good look at the object in the center of the room. It was a cryogenic tube, surrounded by glass walls.

"I knew cryogenics were experimental processes twenty years ago, but I didn't realize they were a viable method of preservation," Thornton remarked. "Is that how you kept him alive?"

Simmons nodded. "Once a new step in our research had been finalized and advanced, we were able to bring the subject out of containment, apply those steps, and put him back on ice before any significant decay." He tapped on his datapad screen. "Everything is green. Looks good, people!"

Thornton held up a hand. "What steps?"

"The steps needed to create the ultimate fighting machine," he said as though this were the most obvious answer in the world. "Cybernetic enhancements, titanium-laced carbon-fiber armor, and my personal favorite, cognitive accelerators in the brain to make effective decisions in the field of battle in a fraction of an instant. That could mean the difference for countless lives. This, of course, took the most time to perfect and is the key to reanimating his brain." Simmons couldn't help but smile at what they had accomplished so far. "This is the most important moment of the last four decades. If his mind can't accept it, he will most likely die of shock and all will have been for naught."

"Very well. Fingers crossed, let's meet him." Thornton adjusted his glasses and his gauntlets. "After all, it's not every day you get to meet your childhood hero."

CHAPTER 3

ARTHUR

"AAAAAAAGGGH!"

Arthur Morris' body seared with flames and frostbite all at once. The pain coursed through every ounce of blood in his body. Every cell felt as if it had been surgically slashed and burned.

"AAAAAAGH, FUCK!"

He had to do something to escape, something to stop the pain. It took all of his might to push open the tube that he found himself trapped inside. He had pushed the door so hard it practically exploded off of whatever this fucking tube was. The cool air steamed as it made contact with the outside atmosphere, billowing out as Arthur stumbled out and onto his feet.

Holy shit, what is this?

Arthur stared around at the antiseptic room, with its metal walls and glass casing.

Wasn't I... dead? What were those hideous animal things? Why does everything hurt so much?

Arthur tripped forward, slamming face first into glass. If nothing else, the pain now centralized in his nose was a distraction from the searing pain everywhere else.

The fog had filled the glass casing outside of the tube he had escaped from. Arthur writhed in pain but managed to stay upright. The pain was starting to subside in his extremities. A voice scratched over what sounded like a loudspeaker. It was muffled at first, but grew clearer. It was repeating his name.

"Thur... Arthur Morris."

Arthur shook his head to clear the cobwebs.

"I can't see!" he yelled. "What's going on?"

"Hold tight, Arthur. We're going to vent the system so you can get a good look," the voice responded.

"Look at what? Who are you?" Arthur put his hand on the glass. The fog in the chamber was too thick to see through. A generator kicked on, and after some creaks in the ventilation shaft, the fog began whirling out of the chamber. Arthur was astonished at what he saw.

The room was full of doctors and scientists in varying shades of lab coats and scrubs. There were armed guards, who were now cocking their assault rifles and staring in his direction.

Directly in front of him was a doctor with a weird transparent tablet, an old guy in a suit smiling like there was no tomorrow, and a large black man in a trench coat who refused to break eye contact. The room was silent for longer than Arthur liked.

"Who. The fuck. Are you?" he puffed. His eyes darted around the room as he grew concerned about his own safety.

The black man stepped forward. "Mr. Morris, my name is Dr. Craig Thornton. This is Dr. Jeffrey Simmons, and this is Mr. Cresher. We represent the Xtremis Program of the United Resistance M—"

"What's wrong? You guys aren't on a first-name basis?"

"Well, aren't you a funny guy?" Cresher grinned. "You can call me Peter."

Arthur hadn't blinked or taken his eyes off of Cresher. He didn't return his smile. There was something about this guy that didn't jive with him. Maybe it was the clean suit while everyone else seemed like they actually worked for a living. He squared his shoulders with Cresher.

"What's going on?" he asked. "Where am I?"

"We're asking the questions here, buddy." Cresher was reveling in the moment. He tapped on the glass like a kid with a fish tank. "You feeling okay? We spent a lot of money to make sure you're comfortable in there. Please tell me you can remember something."

Arthur had to think for a moment. He had flashes of memory, of a life long past.

He was fighting someone. He had weapons.

Weapons he was very proficient with. No, he was pretending to fight someone. Why would he do that?

Cresher noticed his hesitation. "Is it all coming together, pal?"

Arthur remembered there were lots of people watching. There were always people watching.

Everything he did, what for? Did he do something wrong? Then he remembered. His various opponents, the incredibly detailed choreographies, the crowds of people, the cameras, the movie sets, the bright lights. Then he remembered the brightest lights swarming the set on that fateful day.

Arthur's eyes widened. "What the hell was that!? Who are you people? WHERE AM I?"

The security guards took aim, but Dr. Simmons put his hand up to hold their fire. "Hold your fire, he's becoming agitated! Get me a reading!"

"A reading on what? What's happening?" Arthur thought he might be hyperventilating. "It's your lucky day, my friend," Cresher said. "We pulled your body out of the rubble. As destroyed as it was, we basically had to rebuild you from the ground up! It cost the government a pretty penny, but when you've got moves like you do, it's well worth it. The best part is, you are completely upgraded and revamped and you didn't even have to live through the last twenty years to do it!"

Arthur remembered everything, including the painful heat of the moment he and the rest of the world thought was his last. He looked at his face in the faint reflection of the glass, then down at his hands and legs. Before him was a horrifying mess of machinery and organic matter. Arthur screamed in fear, pain, and loss. Twenty years had gone by with those *things* out there.

"Arthur? Arthur? Yoo-hoo?" Cresher snapped his fingers as he continued to talk. "You better pull yourself together and stand up, buddy, because we have lots of work to do. We can't afford to have you falling apart on us before–ACK!"

Arthur had breached the glass, he punched through and grabbed Cresher by the throat. "Shut. Up," Arthur uttered between gritted teeth. His eyes were bloodshot, and he was trembling with rage.

The alarms blared. Thornton stepped in front of Dr. Simmons who tapped furiously at his datapad. Arthur wasn't used to having this kind of strength, but he would have done anything to get this man to shut up. Everyone in the lab was panicking, everyone except Thornton.

That one may be a problem.

The armed guards took aim at Arthur. "Permission to fire, Doc?" one asked.

"Don't shoot, he's still adjusting!" Simmons commanded.

"Sir, he has the VIP by the throat. We just gonna watch him die?"

Despite the situation, Cresher managed to utter something just before Arthur knocked him out by slamming him against the glass. Without thinking or hesitation Arthur smashed through the rest of the enclosure, spewing broken glass through the room. Civilians took cover while the guards stepped up and opened fire. Thornton shoved Dr. Simmons behind a counter.

Arthur reached the first guard within a moment, faster than even he anticipated.

Disarm.

Arthur instinctively knew how to handle an armed opponent. It was even easier now that time had seemed to slow down.

Knee.

Deflect the weapon.

Twist.

Push.

Next target.

Arthur slid from one armed guard to the next, disarming them and putting them down with nonlethal tactics.

Trip.

Throw.

Pull.

This is getting pretty fun. I could do this all—ZZZZZZZZ-ZAAARARARARGH!

A metallic cable had somehow wrapped itself around Arthur and proceeded to deliver a massive electrical shock to his system. He locked up. As much as he tried, he couldn't move anything.

Things were getting hazy again. Before he passed out, all he could see was Thornton standing over him. His trench coat was off, and the cable, attached to a gauntlet, protruded from his weaponized arm. His free hand had another whiplike cable hanging, ready to go. Both cables ran from the gauntlets to what looked like a backpack generating the current all the way into Arthur's body.

"I'm sorry I have to do this. I've been watching your films since I was a kid," Thornton lamented.

"Wait, how old are y—ZZZZAAAAAAGH!!!"

CHAPTER 4

THE NEW WORLD

Arthur woke up on a cot in a cell. He tried to move, but he was chained and padlocked in. He struggled to get free—nothing worked. Arthur wondered what was to come, where he was, who those people were.

Is this hell?

This has to be hell.

I gotta get out of here.

Despite his anguish, Arthur had nearly managed to fall asleep when the latch on the cell door clanged open.

"Shit," he muttered to himself.

The door opened up. Standing there was Thornton flanked by some armed guards.

"Can you guys turn the lights off at least?" Arthur asked. "I'm trying to nap. Can't a guy get some turndown service in here!? This is worse than that time I had to stay at the Embassy Suites in Boston."

The guards hesitated for a moment before Thornton silently signaled for them to leave. "Are you going to behave, or do I have to put you down again?" Thornton brandished a key that gleamed in the light.

Arthur looked at his restraints. "You sure you want to go for round two? I feel much better today." Thornton observed him and tapped his glasses. "What the hell are you doing?"

"Your vitals are remarkably stable, for being in and out of cryo for so long. It's like nothing I've ever seen before. Has anyone talked to you?"

Arthur stopped straining against the chains. He let his head relax onto the pillow and let his eyes stare, unfocused, at the lights overhead. "No, no one has come by. How long has it been? Three days? No one's even dropped any food off. Aren't there laws against this kind of thing?"

"Let me ask you this. Have you been hungry at all?"

"You moron, of co—" Arthur had to think about it. "I guess not. What the hell did you guys do to me?"

"Uh, them, not me," he corrected. "I'm not with these guys. Well, not normally." Thornton sat on the steel chair across from Arthur. "I just joined recently, and I generally avoid dealing with Cresher in any way I can. But, times are tough."

"What do you mean times are tough? Times are always tough." Arthur remembered the flashes of light. "What...What were those things?"

Thornton looked up. He calculated for a second as though deciding whether to continue the conversation. "I guess it's time to let you in on some things."

"I'm cool, Doc. I just need answers."

"Fine, and as a show of good faith, I'll disarm my gear."

Thornton stood up and unlocked Arthur's restraints. The mostly artificial man sat up and stretched his arms and rolled his neck. He got up and walked around, stretched his legs, and glanced out the cell window. Cresher stood talking with the guards. His face was bandaged from their previous encounter, and when he caught a glimpse of Arthur in the window flipping him the bird, he promptly pretended to take a phone call.

Arthur grinned. "I'm gonna have fun messing with that guy. What about you, my man? I showed you mine, you show me yours." Arthur stood with his mechanized arms crossed as he observed Thornton.

Thornton acknowledged him with a nod. He stood up and removed his trench coat. The doctor was in better shape than his title and his demeanor conveyed. On his back was a generator, currently powered off, with cables that ran to the gauntlets on his hands. He smirked. "You already know what these could do. It's what's kept me alive for all these years. It's based off of a design my father had for a lion-taming act, if you can believe it." Thornton shrugged before removing the gauntlets and the power pack. He stopped for a moment and held his palm up, "I wasn't raised in a circus if that's what you're thinking." Arthur shook his head as Thornton continued. The pack unlatched from what looked like a metallic spinal column sticking out from underneath his black tank top.

"Holy shit! That's fantastic. So you took the design and upped the lethality, stuck a robot spine in yourself, and called it a day." Arthur marveled at the equipment. "So you got a code name? Whip Crack? Kunta's Revenge? Something like that?"

"I'm going to pretend you didn't say that. Just call me Thornton, okay?"

"Deal. So, let's talk." Arthur sat back on the bed, and Thornton took the steel chair once more. The two men sat in silence for what felt like hours.

Thornton finally cleared his throat to speak. "Most people call them Demons."

"What?"

"Demons, mythical beasts that came from Hell itself. Or that's the popular story amongst survivors. We don't get a lot of eyewitness reports, but the ones that come through are all very similar."

"Bright lights?" Arthur supplied. "Claws? So many of them?"

"Exactly. They aren't actually from Hell. That would be absurd."

"Are you sure? Are you sure that's the point of absurdity? I don't know where I am or how long it's been. My manager, my agent, my... friends..." Arthur zoned out for a moment of grief as the weight of survival hit him in the chest. "I don't even know how much of me is in here!" His fists clanked against his chest.

Thornton threw his hands up. "Fine, I hear you. They first arrived when the San Andreas Fault cracked open. It was the biggest natural disaster in human history, and has since been dubbed 'The Fracture.' Mankind had no idea what they were, we're still fuzzy about the details, but at least we're getting a good understanding of what they're made of. We classify them by sizes because that seems to be the biggest discrepancy between them all. Iotas, Gammas, Betas, et cetera. The last twenty years have been a concentrated effort to prevent their spread. We have no idea what they want other than to feed on our bodies."

Arthur stared at the floor. "How far has it gotten? How many people have died?"

"Too many to count, but based on where they've popped up, I would say close to about two billion."

"Fucking Christ. Really? Wait, where have they popped up? Not just California?"

"No. Anywhere there has ever been noticeable seismic activity, there have been what essentially are smaller-scale versions of The Fracture. The Himalayas were a particularly tragic event when they spilled into India and China. The American government has pulled as many people east and up north as possible away from their fracture points. The government subsidized German shield technology and placed it all along the Mississippi river up to the Canadian border. Military advances beyond the shield have gone without any positive outcome and such devastation has completely drained resources and assets. Massive sieges and warfare practices have been ineffective. Even black ops missions have failed to even find any rudimentary information on the Demons' motivations. They only chance we have left is us. I wish I could tell you more, but frankly, we don't know much beyond that."

"You guys can't call each other?"

Thornton readjusted on his seat. "That's pretty hard to do when the planet's entire electromagnetic field has been compromised. The Fracture shifted something with the poles, and now every satellite orbiting the planet is useless. At least that's what we've been able to piece together. Radio is the most reliable way to get messages to anyone semi-long distance, but that is sketchy at best. It's part of the reason it's taken this long to get any semblance of unity or a plan to fight back together."

"Between who?"

"Well, that's the part I'm learning, too. There are others, like us."

"Others?"

"Some countries have resources or natural defenses to fight the demons. Russia and Canada are too cold for them to survive for very long. They're from inside the planet's core as far as we can tell, so northern territories are safe havens, but they aren't the most hospitable places to live.

Other countries have developed the technology to fight back. Germany's shield technology has been invaluable to the rest of the world, and they know it. That's where we come in."

"We?"

"We're in the launch stages of what's being called the Xtremis Program. A specialized squad, comprised of augmented individuals such as you and me, coming together from around the world to save it from itself. We're mankind's last line of defense."

"Why me?" Arthur asked. "You could have pulled anybody out of the rubble. I'm just an actor."

Thornton shook his head. "While we both know that's not true, you actually volunteered." Arthur stared at Thornton for a second. "Wait, what? No, I didn't!"

Thornton continued, "It's actually perfect that you did. If you hadn't, I don't know that they would have found a more perfect candidate. You've studied extensively in various forms of martial arts and are proficient in many forms of weaponry."

Arthur sat back and looked up at the ceiling. He had no recollection of signing up for anything like this. He started doubting his own memories now. Thornton carried on, "Which would you say was your favorite weapon to use?"

Arthur thought about it for a moment. He snapped his metal fingers, "You know what was cool? The katana I used in *Virtue Warrior*. That thing was super cool."

Thornton clapped his hands. "I knew it! I loved that movie growing up."

Arthur lowered his gaze to Thornton. "You mentioned that before. You were a fan?"

"Yeah, man! *Virtue Warrior, Honor Amongst Thieves, The Pearson Effect*, all of that was a cornerstone of my existence growing up. I'm incredibly excited to finally be able to—"

A muffled explosion rumbled the room.

"Shit, they're here." Thornton grabbed his whip gauntlets and power pack. Arthur moved to the cell door to look out, and he saw the guards scrambling to get to the surface.

"Hey! Hey! Open up! We're still in here!" Arthur shouted at the guards as they went by.

None of them paid any attention as another explosion rocked the makeshift cell. Arthur continued to bang on the door.

"We've got to get out of here. There's too many civilians at risk." Thornton powered up his backpack and switched on his gauntlets so that the whips were ready to deploy. He pounded on the door himself, but everyone was gone. He calculated for a beat before turning back to Arthur.

"Kick the door down."

"What?" Arthur spluttered.

"Kick the door down! If what they told me about what you can do is accurate, if you kick near the handle we should be able to pry it open."

"You think so?" This sounded too much like movie magic to work in real life, cybernetic enhancements or not.

"Trust me on this."

"I'll give it a shot, but if this is all a hilarious prank to get me to break my foot, I'm going to be really upset."

"Of all the people here, I'm telling you that you can trust me."

"If you say so." Arthur squared up with the door and took a breath.

Thornton stepped back and readied his gauntlets. Arthur looked back at Thornton to give a nod, and Thornton returned the gesture. He prepared his stance and kicked at the handle. The heavy steel door flew off its hinges and slammed across the hallway. Arthur and Thornton stood there wide-eyed, staring at the damage Arthur had done with a basic push kick.

Tears almost welled up in Thornton's eyes. He was trembling with excitement. "We need to test this further, but for now let's go. The armory is this way." He was halfway down the hallway before he realized Arthur wasn't behind him. He turned around and went back to the cell. Arthur was still standing there, looking at the ground. "What's the matter?"

"I'm... not sure. I... don't know what I am."

"Arthur, I know this is all a lot to take in, but I need you to step up right now. For all I know the only thing preventing the demons from overrunning the lab is you and me. After knocking you out a few days back, I'm still operating on a half charge here. I can't do this by myself. I promise we will find all the answers together, but now I need you to kick some ass. Can you do that?" Thornton extended his hand, the gauntlet gleaming in the fluorescent light. Another muffled explosion rumbled overhead.

Arthur nodded. "Yeah... Yeah, let's do it."

FIELD TEST

"You're shitting me, right? You can't bring that thing out into the combat zone right now!" Cresher exclaimed into his radio, trying to maintain his cool despite his facial injuries.

Thornton tapped his earpiece. "Consider it a trial run. How many bogeys are on site?"

"Three Gammas and one Iota. Standard scouting group, they tore through the southeastern gate and seem to have spread out. Two Gammas went north, and the other pair is out on the field. We can only contain them for so long."

"Copy that. I'll take the pair of Gammas, Arthur will get the other two."

"With what? Harsh language? The board hasn't approved armaments yet."

"They don't need to. We made a pit stop on the way up." Thornton gave a thumbs-up to Arthur.

Arthur smirked as he looked up the makeshift elevator shaft. While they were in the armory, Thornton had accessed the equipment made specifically for Arthur. His once vulnerable innards were now protected by a layer of alloys designed to combat the terrestrial threats. On his back was the aforementioned armament of his choice, a katana specially designed for Arthur and his new technological configuration. It was secured in a carbon fiber sheath, magnetized to stay on Arthur's back.

"Just keep security out of the way," the doctor finished. "In fact, send them to back me up on the north wall. Thornton, out."

The elevator came to a halt, and Thornton slammed the gate open. "You ready?"

"As ready as I was made to be."

"Good." Thornton pointed to their left. "Your two are in that direction. I'll probably be needing your help on the north wall once you're finished."

"Whatever, young man. Let's hope I don't fuck this up." Arthur took off in a blink of an eye, following posted signs to the field.

In the middle of the dilapidated stadium turned science lab, two glowing demons shared a meal of one of the security guards. The turf was dug up to make room for experimental pieces of equipment, some of which were covered in blood while others were riddled with bullet holes.

One of the beasts looked to be about the size of a tiger; Arthur figured that one was the Gamma. The other one, the Iota, was the size and shape of a large dog or hyena. The Iota noticed Arthur first as he crept onto the field. It sniffed at the air and growled. Arthur noticed that neither of them had eyes, something he hoped he could use to his advantage. Arthur grabbed a trash bin and hurled it to one side, the metal canister clanging off of some wreckage. The Iota took off towards the noise while the Gamma continued its meal. Arthur clicked open the latch on his sheath. The katana's blade glowed dark red along its edge. Arthur steadied himself. He whistled to get the Iota's attention.

"Hey! Fuckface!"

The Iota howled and took off as fast as it could toward its intended victim. Arthur ran toward it as well. Arthur grasped his katana with both hands and clamped onto the hilt. The Iota leapt toward Arthur.

In one swift movement, Arthur slid underneath the Iota as it sailed over his head. The katana's blade cut through the beast like a hot knife through butter. The Iota was split in half. Its internal fluids spilled onto the turf melting the plastic and rubber into a hot orange pool. Arthur whipped his katana to get the remnants off of the blade. The bits of what looked like embers of lava cooled off into harmless rocks as they hit the ground.

The Gamma crashed through lab equipment right behind Arthur, who took off running. The Gamma howled as it gave chase. Arthur formulated a plan as he ran. His reflexes were so fast it was as if time had slowed down to give him a breather.

I got you.

Arthur veered to the right sideline wall and allowed the Gamma to catch up. The glowing monstrosity pounced, but Arthur sidestepped the beast's massive claws and decapitated it. The head bounced and spewed the glowing liquid, melting the turf. The Gamma's body did the same as it fell to the ground, lifeless. Some of the spewing magma had gotten on Arthur's armor. The smell of burning metal tipped him off to the fact that he was on fire. Arthur managed to put out the flames quickly after he panicked more than he would care to admit.

"I'm glad nobody saw that," Arthur muttered to himself before taking off in Thornton's direction. He hoped that his new friend hadn't been killed yet; he was the only ally he had in this new world.

At the same time, Thornton actually had his hands full with the remaining Gamma. The other's body was lying on the ground, its neck twisted and broken. The surviving Gamma had Thornton pinned against the concrete wall, though he had managed to lodge one gauntlet in the beast's mouth and was trying to defend against its sharp claws.

Blood dripped from his forehead onto his face as he gritted his teeth and pushed back against the monster. He could feel the heat from the Gamma's innards bearing down on him. Suddenly the pressure was all gone. Thornton fell to his knees and caught a breather. The Gamma, surprised by the mass that had just collided into it, scrambled to get back on to its feet.

Arthur helped Thornton to stand and gave him a pat on the shoulder. "Not bad, old man," Thornton said. "The other two taken care of?"

"Yeah, they won't be bothering us." Arthur kept his eyes on the Gamma who was gearing up to pounce again.

Thornton extended his whips but didn't power them up. "I've got an idea."

"Yeah?"

"Slingshot special, he won't see it coming."

The two exchanged nods. Thornton stepped in front of Arthur. He threw his whips back and latched onto Arthur's arms. The Gamma let forth an ungodly screech and began to charge.

"GO!" Thornton yelled. He retracted his whips and slung Arthur towards the Gamma. Arthur tucked his body in and held out his katana with both hands, creating a destructive buzz saw that sliced the Gamma completely in half. Arthur landed in a crouch and cleaned his blade in one flick of the wrist. The hot blood of the beast boiled on the concrete until it cooled into a pile of rocks. Arthur spun his katana a couple of times before putting it back in the sheath. Arthur paused for a moment to process what happened. It took every servo and muscle inside his body to have the self-restraint to not jump in the air celebrating how cool he thought that was.

Thornton was having an even harder time restraining himself.

Almost instantly, the security guards barreled into the passageway, weapons drawn and pointed directly at Arthur. Cresher and Dr. Simmons followed behind them. Arthur snapped to attention and prepared himself for another fight. The guards spread out in formation, but Thornton stepped up in front of Arthur and held his arms out to shield him.

"HOLD YOUR FIRE!" Thornton bellowed.

"Step aside, Craig!" replied Cresher. "That thing needs to go back into containment."

"He's not the threat here. The demons were neutralized, mostly by him."

One by one, the guards took notice of the demons turned headless rock formations Arthur and Thornton had taken down. Dr. Simmons grabbed his datapad out of his satchel and tapped at the screen. He smiled excitedly and walked up to the pair.

"Dr. Thornton, you have to look at this information. He performed well beyond expectations.

The experiment was a complete success!" Simmons reported. He looked back at Cresher. "It worked! We have a chance!" Simmons hugged the nearest guard while the rest of them lowered their weapons.

Thornton breathed a sigh of relief.

Arthur released his grip on the katana, walked up to the nearest guard, and shook his hand. "Hi, I'm Arthur Morris. Pleased to meet you! Thank you for not shooting me in the face. Which, to my knowledge is my only weak spot." The guards gathered around to see his robotic functions and to talk to the half-man, half-machine. Cresher pushed his way past them and got in Thornton's face.

"You son of a–! Listen, Craig, bubelah. I'm happy that the experiment worked, I really am. But seeing as you're now in charge of field ops on this gig, I need you to make sure that our new toy here does as he's told and stays in line. If not, and he decides to go Skynet on us? It's your responsibility to put him down. Got it?"

"I hear you," Thornton acknowledged.

"Good!" Cresher stormed down the hallway, and Thornton watched Arthur socializing with the guards. Thornton hoped that he wouldn't have to do anything to hurt the man he grew up idolizing, since he now owed him his very life.

CHAPTER 6

PROOF POSITIVE

Arthur, Thornton, Dr. Simmons, and Cresher were all strapped into the cargo hold of a C-130 Hercules cargo plane. Security personnel rounded out the cabin along with several large crates of lab equipment and supplies, the United States' contribution to the Xtremis program.

"Is this all?" Thornton asked Cresher.

"No, this is just so we can get RoboMan here up and running," Cresher replied. "This is all the equipment to maintain and upgrade him as time and battles wear on. The U.S. is supplying soldiers and equipment at the F.O.B."

"Uh, Upgrades?" Arthur spoke up.

"Yes, previously, we were concerned with the stability of your mind making the transition into this new world." Dr. Simmons held up his datapad. "Now that you are here and combat- tested, we can focus on making you the ultimate weapon against the demons."

"Great. No pressure there." Arthur shook his head. It was almost unnoticeable as the entire aircraft shook with the turbulent storm. "Where is home base?"

"Glad you asked," said Cresher with a smile. The smile did nothing to hide the bandage on his nose. Arthur was particularly proud of that. "We're going to switch to a chopper near the Gulf of California and then we're heading out to sea. It's the safest place against the demons.

Specifically operations are launching from the USS *Ronald Reagan*." The plane groaned and croaked against the stormy night sky.

"We are actually going to make it there, right?" Thornton asked, barely looking up from his datapad. Cresher was already fast asleep wearing a crushed velvet blindfold.

Arthur looked at Dr. Simmons who shrugged. "Now, Arthur. Once we get situated, and you get a free moment, I would like to do some tests with you, just to get an idea of what you are capable of. Would that be okay?"

"Sure, Dr. Simmons. Thanks for actually asking," Arthur said as he looked over at Cresher. Cresher was peeking out from under his blindfold and gave him the middle finger before going back to sleep. "Classy."

The intercom scratched to life. "This is your captain. We're approaching demonic airspace.

Prep for lockdown and potential enemy fire."

The cabin lights went red, and everyone double-checked their security straps. Cresher didn't move.

"Um, what's going on?" Arthur asked.

"Don't worry, this is standard procedure," Dr. Simmons reassured him. "Most of the time, the demons don't even notice airborne vehicles unless it's out of self-defense. If we fly high enough, they would barely see us, much less take us down."

Arthur looked around. He seemed to be the only one concerned about the potential of going down in a fireball of death. "You guys have been through a lot, haven't you?"

"Of course we have. But that's what led us to you." Simmons gave him a warm smile.

"I just... what the hell is that?" Arthur noticed something out of his view port window. Down beneath the aircraft was a wasteland of destruction. Buildings were destroyed, blown apart and crumbling. Glyphs of light shone as the demons ran unchecked through the ruins. A flock of winged lights circled over an opening in the center of the city.

Thornton looked up from his datapad. "Phoenix, Arizona."

"What?!"

"You see that giant, glowing ravine? It's one of many that opened up around the world. Little mini-fractures."

"Do they always make the city end up like this?"

"No. Various cities, countries and governments around the globe have had varying degrees of success. Others, such as the entire West Coast... Well, you can see. Of course, it is a giant sieve in the ground. There isn't a whole lot mankind can do to prevent that."

"My god." Arthur looked down as far as he could into the ravine as they flew over it. Even at their high altitude, he could see the crevasse in the center of the city. Lava and smoke billowed out like veins stretching across the landscape. The light from the canyon was so intense it felt like he was staring into the planet's core itself.

Once they got to the landing strip somewhere west of Sonora, California, the crew began loading up several Chinook helicopters with the lab equipment they had brought. Dr. Simmons had suggested they do some exercises out on the tarmac during their down time. Arthur agreed, wanting to stretch his legs a little bit, and proceeded down the ramp and out into the night.

Some of the guards had warmed up to Arthur. They had gathered around to watch the exercise, some were even taking bets. Before Arthur lay a set of armor they had pulled from the stock they were bringing. They had set it up like a scarecrow or a man-shaped target. One of them, as a joke, put a blindfold on the makeshift mannequin.

"Settle down, settle down!" Dr. Simmons calmed the ever-growing crowd of soldiers and personal security. "Okay, Mr. Morris here was an accomplished actor and a prolific martial artist with high efficiency in multiple disciplines. Then, we got ahold of him and did our best to make him even better! With good old fashioned American ingenuity, we have made Arthur Morris a killing machine! "

The crowd of guards roared with approval. Arthur put a hand up to acknowledge their cheers.

Even though it was all still new to him, if there was one thing he knew how to do, it was entertaining an audience while being wildly uncomfortable on the inside. Dr. Simmons tapped away at his datapad. Thornton and Cresher grabbed a seat on some nearby crates to watch the show.

"First up! Soldier, hand him your combat knife," Simmons directed. The soldier standing next to him complied with the order and handed Arthur his personal combat knife. It was heavy and serrated on one side. Arthur looked at the knife, then at his target. Then he turned to face the crowd and held the knife up by the blade. A hushed murmur came from the crowd. Simmons held an arm out and lightly pushed himself and another soldier away from what was about to happen.

Arthur looked at Thornton and gave a wink. Thornton raised an eyebrow in response. Then, Arthur threw the knife straight up in the air. The knife flew upwards, end over end. Arthur kicked up with his left leg, throwing his body completely upside down before bringing up his right foot to connect perfectly with the knife's hilt, sending it speeding toward the mannequin. He flipped completely and landed precisely on one knee, wowing the audience of soldiers before him. As he took in their applause, he looked back at the mannequin behind him. The knife was sticking out of its face. The crowd went crazy as Arthur tried to keep his co/mposure and not seem as giddy as he was on the inside that he just pulled off a stunt like that.

"Ho-ly shit," Cresher remarked.

"Told you, he's good," Thornton replied.

"Ever the performance artist, Mr. Morris!" Dr. Simmons exclaimed as he got the soldiers to calm down. "Next test, here's a nine-millimeter. Your opponent is bearing down on you, subdue him."

"Pssh. Subdue." Arthur snorted. Thornton took notice of that reaction and fixed his glasses. He tapped a button on the side to take a closer look. His lenses zoomed in as Thornton got a look at Arthur's face.

He's reveling in this. He loves it.

Arthur took the weapon from the doctor. The crowd moved back, giving him more space to work with. He took a breath, and then started spinning the pistol on his finger. "Yeehaw, boys! I learned this on the set of *Blue Noon*," he explained. "It took me six weeks to get it down with the coach on set. Hey, doc, do I have a RoboCop leg? Like with the holster?" He gestured to his leg with his free hand while the gun was spinning around. He looped it around his head and behind his back.

"We can look into that for an upgrade if you'd like," replied the doctor.

"Sweet." Arthur, in one smooth movement, turned back towards the mannequin, released the safety, and pulled the trigger three times. The mannequin had three fresh bullet holes smoking in its face around the knife.

The now larger crowd of soldiers whooped and hollered at the sight of it.

"This guy is unreal."

"There's no way! That's gotta be like bullshit."

"What did I tell you, *vato*? This dude's legit."

Dr. Simmons signaled for them to be quiet. "One last test, with your weapon of choice. Your katana."

The crowd got extra excited, even though many of them stepped as far back as they could for this display.

"Oh, and one more thing." The doctor whispered something into Arthur's ear.

Arthur's eyes lit up. "Are you serious? Ho ho, man. This is awesome. Step back, folks."

He squared up about thirty feet away from his mannequin rival. His hand gripped the hilt of his blade as he crouched into a battle-ready stance. Slowly he removed his blade, showing off the dark red glow from its edge. Then he flipped a switch he hadn't noticed before on the hilt, separating the sword into two. The crowd oohed and ahhed at the new configuration.

Arthur spun each blade individually back and forth. Then he crossed his arms as he spun, creating a figure eight of death. He leapt towards his target and, in one motion, bounded and corkscrewed in the air behind it, both blades at its neck. Swift and precise, he sliced the mannequin's head off and into the air. Arthur's eyes never left the head as he recombined the blades into one. He sheathed the katana before catching the head by the hilt of the knife that was still in its face.

The crowd of soldiers nearly lost their minds. "Wow," said Cresher. "Now he's just showing off."

"Yeah, he is. Wouldn't be on the team if he didn't have a bit of that American swagger," Thornton replied as he adjusted his glasses.

"Exactly. Not only are we putting him front and center, but I'm also going to make sure the entire planet knows that our guy is *the* guy. Make sure there is an American flag on his chest somewhere."

"Bloody hell." Thornton rolled his eyes.

CHAPTER 7

XTREMIS

The Boeing CH-47 Chinook helicopter carrying the VIPs was the first to land on the *Reagan*.

Dr. Simmons stepped off with Cresher, flanked by several scientists taking the lab equipment somewhere below deck. Thornton and Arthur stepped off the ramp with a squad of personal security assigned to make sure Arthur wouldn't go haywire. They had all seemed to lighten up after the display Arthur made at the transition point, and universally agreed that he wasn't a threat. The ship's captain, a sprightly, older gentleman in a clean Navy officer's uniform, greeted them along with a group of naval officers stationed on the ship. He reached out and shook Thornton's hand.

"Dr. Thornton, Captain Alan Tobin, pleasure to have you aboard. This is my XO, Commander Gary Fletcher."

"How do you do, gentlemen?" Thornton shook the XO's hand as well. Fletcher, noticing the gauntlet Thornton was equipped with, shot a glance to his captain.

"Relax, Gary. It's not the strangest thing we've seen on the ship. Dr. Thornton here is part of the Xtremis crew. From what I hear, he's now in charge of it."

"That's right. I'd like to get Arthur here down to the hangar to meet the rest of the group. He is the United States' representative after all." He gestured for Arthur to join them.

"Hello sirs, I would first like to thank you for your service to this country." Arthur spoke as respectfully as he could muster.

Fletcher was taken aback, as he recognized Arthur right away. "Arthur Morris? From *King Fu* and *Process of Elimination*?"

Arthur blushed a little. "Yes, that's me."

"Oh my god, I thought you were dead!"

"I was!"

Fletcher shook his head. "Your movies helped me get through OCS. I'm honored to have you on board."

"Well, thank you for having us. I can't wait to get started."

"Uh, speaking of which," Thornton interjected with a wave of his datapad, "we should head down to the hangar and meet the rest of the group. Arthur, let's go."

"You got it, boss man. Hey, thanks again, you guys."

"Oh, no problem. We're ready to get this fight underway." Fletcher shook Arthur's hand one more time before regrouping with the other naval officers.

"This way, Arthur." He followed Thornton down to the hangar bay. "Training exercises are taking place at the moment. It'll give you a good idea about our partners' capabilities."

"Do you know any of these people?"

"I've been looking over their records, and there are some remarkable people here." Thornton opened the latch to a bulkhead leading into the hangar. "You didn't think we were the only special ones, did you?"

Inside, the hangar was retrofitted to be a training area. It currently held soldiers, sailors, and scientists, lined up along the sides, waiting for something to happen. Standing among them was the first on Thornton's list.

"Hans? Hans Schreiber?" The large blonde man turned around when he heard someone calling his name.

"Ja?" he said with a thick German accent.

"Hello! My name is Dr. Craig Thornton. I'm going to be spearheading the Xtremis project from here on out."

"Oh! Ja! I was wondering when you would get here. It is a pleasure to finally meet you! And who might this be?" He pointed to Arthur, and Arthur noticed that, up close, he was much bigger than he had originally thought.

"This is Arthur Morris, our asset from the U.S."

"Wunderbar! Welcome aboard, ha ha!" He grabbed Arthur and gave him a massive hug, lifting him up off the floor as he did.

Arthur wondered if he would need repairs after this. "It's—great to meet you too!" he managed to strain the words out.

Hans finally put him back down. "You two are just in time! The show is about to start."

"Show?" Arthur asked.

"The sisters are sparring. No limits!"

Thornton tapped at his datapad. "The Sakurai sisters? Oh, I need to see this." Thornton secured a front-row spot, pushing his way past a couple of sailors.

Arthur sized up Hans; he didn't seem like someone like himself, someone augmented. Hans was, although rather large, just a normal guy to him.

"Hans?"

"Yes, my friend?"

"What can you do?"

"Me? Ho ho, nothing. But my suit of armor is going to be what keeps us all alive."

"Armor, huh? It seems like that doesn't help the group so much as it helps yourself."

"Well, if you'd like, I would love to show it off one on one." Hans smiled his big, toothy smile.

Arthur was intrigued. *This guy is hiding something, but I'm sure I can take him.*

"You're on, my friend. What are the rules to this little sparring session?"

Hans' smile grew even bigger. "First to immobilize their opponent wins. You may use whatever you want, tactics, weapons, insults, whatever it takes."

Arthur couldn't help but laugh at the other man's bravado. "I like you, Hans. You're all right."

"You may not like me after our training."

"Well, I'm prepared to pick you up after I win and shake your hand."

Hans laughed his big, hearty laugh. "This will be fun! I cannot wait to get started!"

Fuck you. Arthur was getting worked up now. *What's this guy's problem? Nobody's this nice.*

He decided to change the subject. "So what can you tell me about the Sushi girls?"

"The Sakurais are Japan's greatest assets," Hans said. "They singlehandedly saved their homeland from many threats. Demons, Invasions, even a Tsunami."

"What? H-How?" Arthur tried to imagine how these two girls could possibly do so much, one on one with demons like the ones he fought back in Texas. "And you're going to make them fight each other?"

"It was their idea! They trained like this every day in Japan, honing their skills for the day they would be needed." Hans shrugged. "It's not a bad regimen. It's not like the Demons practice or have safety briefings."

A murmur ran throughout the crowd of sailors and soldiers. The sisters had arrived to a wave of cheers, catcalls, and whistles. Yoko and Mia Sakurai entered the hangar geared up for battle. Mia had her hair tied up in a neat bun. Her blue armor was form-fitting and very light. Her blue eyes shimmered as she glared at her opponent. She wore a pair of gloves that were secured to her sleeves. The upper-body portion of her outfit looked to be lined with fur, and she looked as if she were ready to go on a skiing expedition. Besides her cargo belt, she only carried with her a metallic staff that was insulated most of the way up to a glass point. On her staff was a guard built specifically for her hand to grab hold and operate it.

Her twin sister, Yoko, looked nearly identical to Mia, yet she was the opposite of her in almost every way. Her eyes were an unnatural shade of red. Yoko liked to keep her hair down and free, as free as her neck-length hair was going to be. Her reddish-pink armor was also very light but seemed to have different functionality. Her cargo belt seemed to be damaged and blackened, almost dirty. In fact, all of her armor looked to have a thin layer of soot on it. Arthur surmised that she looked like she had been at the front line of every battle against the demons since The Fracture. Her gloves looked toasted with scorch marks, but had two sharp metallic blades coming out of the wrist on both sides. There was a nozzle attached to a tube leading to a pack she was carrying, not unlike Thornton's power pack.

The women were twins, but for some reason, Arthur couldn't let his attention move away from Mia. He was transfixed. He hadn't even thought about women since he had woken up. In fact, he wasn't even sure he could—

"AAGH!" The battle cries of the sisters shook Arthur out of his train of thought. Yoko swung her wrist blades at Mia who deflected with her staff.

Back and forth, they advanced their position and retreated, both going full force with the power of their swings.

Arthur leaned over to Hans. "Are they actually trying to kill each other?"

Hans leaned over to Arthur. "Let me ask you this: will the demons know the difference?

They are always trying to kill you, so why practice for anything less?"

Arthur hadn't thought of that. Then he thought about ways to kill Hans, if only for a moment. The sisters continued their battle. Mia managed to get some distance between herself and her sister by kicking Yoko away. Yoko tumbled backwards and rolled back onto her feet. She looked pissed off and ready to almost kill Mia. With another yell she flipped a switch on her utility belt, and a plume of flame shot from the nozzle on her wrist towards Mia. Mia grabbed her staff and spun it in front of her towards the flame. The end of the staff lit up in a blue aura that pushed the flames back.

"Sweet mother of Christ!" Arthur exclaimed.

"There it is! Yeah!" Hans cheered along with the rest of the crowd. Thornton watched silently and made notes on his datapad while the battle raged on. Flames spewed off of a slowly forming ice wall.

Mia shouted as she slammed her staff down, and a blue pulse put out the flames. The blue pulse-wave also left Yoko frozen to the floor, as her boots were covered in ice. The crowd roared with approval. Mia smiled and waved at the crowd as she made her way over to her sister, who was struggling to get free of the ice block that had formed around her ankles. Mia came over and helped her out with one strike from her staff. The ice shattered and Yoko stepped out, huffing and puffing, upset that she had lost the training session. She stared at Mia for a moment, her fists balled up and clenched. Mia didn't break her gaze with her sister until Yoko let out a snicker.

She couldn't hold it in anymore and just outright laughed. Mia broke and also laughed. Together they stood there laughing until Yoko had to wipe away a tear. The two hugged and waved to their audience.

Mia caught a glimpse of Hans—pretty easy seeing as he towered over everybody with his massive frame, even outside of his armor—but next to him were two faces she didn't recognize. They stood out among the uniformed men and women, a black man with glasses and a trench coat and another man. He looked American as far as she could tell but there was something not right, something artificial about him.

Arthur mistook her curiosity for flirtation. She didn't take her eyes off of him as their group approached the sisters. Arthur flipped his hair back, extended his hand, and tried to speak in his most suave and sultry voice. "Hi, I'm Arthur Morris. That was... quite impressive."

Mia giggled at this poor attempt at flirting. "Thank you," she said. "Welcome."

Yoko saw this and stepped in, red eyes flaring as she shoved Arthur aside and brandished her wrist blades while cursing at him in Japanese. "You son of a bitch, step off before I cut your dick off!"

Arthur put his hands up and took a step back. Mia held Yoko back and said something quietly to her sister in Japanese. "Calm down, he's harmless. Besides, I know who to call if I'm ever in trouble."

"Fine, just make sure you let him know, I'm not in control of what happens if he touches you. Dick. Off."

Arthur was wondering what was happening. Yoko sounded angry. "Uh, everything okay?"

"Oh, it is fine," Mia said, "she's just, uh, protective of me!"

Thornton interjected. "From the looks of it, you can protect your-self." He bowed to them.

Mia and Yoko both returned his bow. "Thank you, we love that every-one enjoys our practice sessions," Mia said. "You are Mr. Thornton, yes?"

"Dr. Thornton," he corrected. "I'm going to be heading up the Xtremis project for the foreseeable future. But you can call me Craig if you like."

The sisters looked at each other. Yoko made an attempt to say it in her thick, Japanese accent: "Curegu." Mia elbowed her in the ribs. Hans slapped Arthur on the back so hard he nearly lost his footing.

"Aha! Arthur, it is time! I'm off to prepare for battle! Feel free to use the bathroom or grab a drink of water, whatever you need to do to prepare."

"Yeah, thanks, Hans," Arthur answered with an insincere smile. He couldn't wait to show him who was boss. Arthur turned his atten-tion back to Mia and Yoko. "That was really something, you two. I can see why Japan sent you."

"We take pride in our training, and we share a passion for protect-ing the world," Mia said. Yoko motioned that she was leaving. Mia responded with a nod and held up her fist. Yoko fist-bumped her and went on her way, retracting her wrist blades and removing her pack. Mia looked back at Arthur. "It was a pleasure getting to know you. I'm sorry for what is about to happen."

Arthur's face dropped. He was disappointed that she had so little faith in him. She smiled at him as she mingled with the crowd of sail-ors congratulating her on her victory and shaking her gloved hands.

"What's up with the gloves?" Arthur said to Thornton.

"I'm not sure actually. I only have rudimentary files on them and their accomplishments." Thornton pointed to his datapad. "Every-thing Hans said is true: they repelled many invaders both demonic and human. They singlehandedly led the charge of Japanese forces against North Korea when the Koreans blamed the Japanese for the Demons."

"And the tsunami?"

"Also true, Mia faced the tsunami herself and, with the help of that staff designed specifically for her abilities, froze part of the ocean itself long enough for evacuations to finish."

"Wow, what else is there?"

"That's the problem. That's it."

Until now, Arthur had seen Dr. Thornton as an unending fountain of knowledge. "How?" he spluttered.

"I don't know, it's all classified by the Japanese government," the doctor said. "There's something here among the files, but it's going to take some time for me to decrypt it. Whatever it is, I need to know and I need to determine if it is going to affect the plan of attack."

"Well, let me know if I can help in any way."

"There is actually something you can do for me, Arthur." He tapped his lip. "Dr. Simmons has been working on the second phase of your weapons and abilities. Maybe he can give you some central processing access."

"That... actually sounds painful. Listen, Doc, I don't know. From what I've been told, I only have my brain and not much else. I don't know if I want you guys rooting around in there."

"Fine, but you should talk to Dr. Simmons after this."

"After what?"

"After Hans." Thornton pointed behind Arthur to the hangar elevator. Normally reserved for transporting aircraft to and from the top deck, right now, it served as a platform for Hans and his personal set of armor. It looked heavy and impenetrable, and yet Hans could move freely in it.

On his arms were two electromagnetic generators, and on his right shoulder was something that looked like a two-pronged heavy-rail cannon. He posed as the elevator slowly brought him down. He pointed out to the crowd of onlookers and then slowly pointed at Arthur as the elevator came to a halt.

"Oh, fuck me, really?" Arthur slumped.

Thornton patted him on the back and leaned in close. "Well, good luck, old man."

"Thanks." Arthur watched Thornton blend into the audience that was now raucous for the next fight on the card.

He could hear Hans stomp up to him and boom a laugh. "Are you ready, my new friend?"

Arthur did his best to grit his teeth into a grin. "Any time, pal! You want me to go easy on you? Seems like you've got a lot going on with your getup there."

"Ohh, my Panzer suit is one of a kind. It is so advanced, I have to give you a break. So I will not be using the cannon." Hans responded through the speaker system in his helmet. He unlatched the shoulder cannon and dropped it onto the deck with a thud.

"How thoughtful. We're just trying to pin each other, right?"

"Ja, that is how it is done." Hans loosened up and stretched. It had been some time since he last had to wear the suit. The armor looked worn and battle-scorched, possibly from years of battling the Demons.

Arthur limbered up as well. "You ready, big boy?" he said as he leaned into a stretch. "Ja, whenever you are."

Hans got into his battle stance. He bent his knees slightly and crossed his arms so that the electromagnets powered up. Arthur prepared himself for a fight. He crouched low and took his katana out of its sheath. The crowd oohed at the sight of the awesome weapon.

Arthur couldn't see Hans' face, but he imagined that he would be impressed, too.

In the crowd, Thornton pulled up Hans' file on his datapad. His eyes widened as he looked at Arthur, who wasn't taking his eyes off of Hans. "Arthur! Don—"

But Arthur didn't hear the rest of Thornton's command. He took off at high speed, as fast as he could, toward Hans. Hans held his ground and didn't flinch. Underneath the armor his smile was as big as ever. Arthur was still running at full speed across the hangar at his target, sword drawn. Hans still wasn't moving when Arthur leapt off of his feet and bounded off of Hans' forearms, straight up into the air. He demonstrated some of his agility to the crowd with a gainer somersault, and then whipped his katana around to point it downward at Hans. Arthur let out a battle cry as he came down with his katana.

The electromagnetic generators on Hans' crossed arms powered up, and an electrical current surged and sparked around the coils. Arthur only had enough time to realize that there was no way he was getting through.

The coils pulsed as they repelled Arthur's body into the roof of the hangar. He hit the ceiling with a resounding clang as his katana hurtled end over end, ultimately impaling itself into the bulkhead. Arthur fell limply to the hangar floor as Hans stepped out of the way. His body was scorched and smoking as he tried to shake off the effects of the electrocution.

Hans put one foot on Arthur and put his arms in the air, signaling victory. Arthur strained to move the massive, armored boot, but no luck. He resigned himself to his defeat. The crowd let out a disappointed murmur and started to head back to their workstations.

"Are you all right, my friend?" Hans directed the question toward

Arthur as he lifted his boot off of him.

"Yeah, Hans. I'm okay. I'm sure girls weren't watching, so I'm okay." Arthur gave him a thumbs-up as he peeled himself off of the floor.

"Good to hear!" Hans lifted Arthur off of the ground with a big hug, popping his vertebrae from lumbar to thoracic.

Thornton walked over to the two of them, waving away the stench of scorched metal. "That was enlightening," he said while he huffed the smoke out of his nose. "I can't say I've seen anything quite like this. How many of these suits were manufactured by the German military?"

"Exactly zero." Hans removed his helmet. He hadn't broken a sweat. He ran his gauntleted hand through his high and tight blonde haircut. "The German military has been trying to get the designs for the Panzer since my father invented it. He never relinquished the plans even after he died. I am now the carrier of my father's legacy."

"Is that why Germany sent you here?" Arthur asked.

"Heh, yes. If I die out here, they will have the designs that they want. If I survive the mission, they will leave me be." Hans looked at the ground, shuffling in his suit as he spoke.

Thornton tapped on his datapad a few more times. "Arthur, there's one more for us to meet.

Hans, would you care to introduce us to Mr. Walker?"

Hans awoke out of it. "Excellent! Braxton is most probably up on the flight deck. We will take the elevator. Follow me." The three moved to the lift that Hans had used on his way down. Arthur felt embarrassed and maybe a bit humbled as he followed behind the giant. Despite his shame, he was glad he was to have Hans on their team.

As the lift rumbled into action, Thornton pulled up Walker's file on his datapad. "Oh, my."

"What? What's his deal?" Arthur looked over Thornton's shoulder.

"Walker is a mercenary, highly proficient in firearms and explosives."

"Okay, awesome, I feel like we need that. What's the problem?" Arthur insisted.

Hans spoke up. "Braxton is from Australia." It was the only time Arthur had seen Hans without a smile on his face.

"Well, that explains the lethality, but so what? Australia? What's the big deal?" Hans looked at Arthur and Thornton incredulously.

"Does he not know?" Hans raised his eyebrows at Thornton, who stared back blankly before realizing.

"Oh! Right. Sorry, he's new." Thornton turned to Arthur. "There is no more Australia."

"What? H-How? You should really not bury the lede if a whole country is missing."

"You remember the tsunami that Japan stopped? Australia wasn't so lucky. Between more fractures, demons, flooding, and earthquakes, Australia became uninhabitable. Then, in a last- ditch effort, the Australian government tried to purge their lands of the demons in one move. They nuked themselves trying to get rid of them. It didn't work, and now there's nothing left there. The fracture has had all kinds of ramifications across the planet. It's why we've all been brought here to take back the planet."

"Jesus." Arthur couldn't believe what he was hearing. He had thought that the amount of demon territory in the States was bad, but he couldn't imagine if the US was gone completely, in the push of a button. Arthur got depressed thinking about it, especially considering the fact that he didn't have anybody from his past life here in what he considered the future.

"Cheer up, my friends. We are here together now. We are now family... together." Hans slapped Thornton and Arthur on the back, and the lift came to a halt.

At the end of the flight deck, a man laid on his stomach in a prone position Arthur recognized as a standard shooting position. Manning a Barrett M107 .50-caliber rifle, Braxton Walker was looking down the scope while aiming the rifle out to sea.

"Mr. Walker," Thornton called to him.

"Shh." Walker held up a finger, pointed at a bird out at sea, then adjusted his sights. Arthur could see the bird he pointed to was alone and struggling to stay aloft.

"Oh no," Arthur uttered. Walker's eyes adjusted and zoomed in. The details on the bird's wings were as clear to him as if the bird were right in front of him. He held his breath and gave the trigger a slight squeeze. With a loud *thunk,* the rifle fired a round, and in an instant the bird disappeared in a pink mist.

"Ugh." Arthur squirmed.

"Problem?" Walker grunted more than spoke.

Arthur, despite all of his abilities and augments, felt intimidated. He knew what kind of damage a rifle like that could do, and he knew that someone like Walker wasn't someone to have a grudge with. "No, no problem. How far was that shot?" Arthur asked, hoping to pivot the conversation.

"About four hundred yards, give or take." Walker spat on the deck. He squinted at Arthur who got a good look at his eyes finally. They were metallic blue with what looked like a camera lens in both eyes. "You the other guys we're waiting on?"

"That's right," Thornton spoke up. "I'm Dr. Craig Thornton, and this is Arthur Morris."

"Great. I'll see you all at the briefings." Walker grabbed his rifle and pushed past the group.

Hans halted him by putting an armored hand on his shoulder.

"Walker, please. We are all on the same side here."

"Less targets for me. Welcome to Xtremis, try not to die." Walker pulled himself away from the giant Kraut and headed below deck into the briefing room.

OPERATION FOOTHOLD

Arthur yawned as he sat in the briefing room. It had been converted from a squadron's mission briefing room with enough desks to fulfill an entire fighter squadron.

Dr. Simmons gave Arthur a nudge to the ribs to attempt to get him to focus. It did nothing for Arthur, but Simmons did regret it immediately as he hit his funny bone on the cyborg's armor.

Hans took a seat on Arthur's other side with his regularly large grin on his face. The sisters sat next to each other in the aisle across from them. Walker sat on top of the desk in the back corner against the wall, picking at his fingernails with a bowie knife. Thornton walked in with his datapad and stepped up to the podium, while Cresher slipped in behind him.

"Good evening, everyone. It's good to see you here as one team. As you all know, we've brought the world's finest assets together in one bid to fight back against the Demons and take back the planet. Tomorrow is the first step towards that goal."

He tapped at his datapad, and a topographical map of San Diego was projected into the air.

Various marks and indicators highlighted pockets of Demon activity and the location of the fracture through the center of the city. "Here we have Coronado, the Gaslamp Quarter, and the former naval air station. They are priorities in our efforts to take back the city. We need to eliminate enemy presence in these points before we meet up near the baseball stadium, to establish a foothold for the troops to move in. From there we will evac using the choppers and arrive back here to restock and rest up, should everything go according to plan."

"In what order are we taking the objectives? They seem like big spaces to cover," Hans asked.

"I'm glad you asked." Thornton highlighted the sections of the map. "We're going to take them all at the same time."

The group groaned, and Arthur decided to speak up. "The same time? How?"

"We're going to split into three groups, integrating our abilities where they will be the most useful. Walker will be with the helicopter squadron taking the naval air station. It's flat, and the buildings aren't very tall. Walker, can you shoot from a moving helicopter?" Everyone looked to the back of the room.

Walker lifted the rim of his hat and glared at Thornton for what felt like an eternity. "If the pilot can keep it steady enough, sure. I'll take the base."

"Good. Next, the Gaslamp Quarter." He looked at the Sakurai sisters. "That's where you two will come in. The Demons are the heaviest in that area, and since you have the most experience in combating them, you ought to be able to handle that. Right?"

They nodded their confirmation. "You can count on us," Mia replied.

"For Coronado, Hans, Arthur, and myself are going to take the island. It used to be tourist destinations and military housing. This will be the insertion point for troops and supplies from the *Reagan*."

"Very good. What happens when we meet at the stadium?" asked Hans.

"We hope our backup arrives in time to take us back to the ship to resupply and prepare for our next mission, which will be going down into the fracture to see what we can find. Ultimately, I feel like we can find the key to beating the Demons down there. If all else fails, we can bring it down from the inside."

"Can we try to avoid that for now? We don't have any way of evacuation if it crumbles down on top of us." Arthur pointed out. "Unless you gave me a jetpack I don't know about." Simmons shook his head. Arthur was relieved and yet slightly disappointed. Simmons wrote a note down. *Jetpack?* And underlined it.

"I have jet boots. At the very least, I can blow the canyon and make my escape." Hans smiled.

"Of course he does," Arthur whispered to Dr. Simmons. "I've got a question, if Hans' suit is so awesome, which by the way no offense, it is super awesome. If it's so awesome why cant he just blast every demon away with that huge cannon that totally isn't compensating for anything by the way." He said louder to the group, ensuring Hans heard him.

"The Panzer suit is impressive technology, but his shoulder cannon doesn't do well on closer encounters. Which, as you've seen, is the Demons' entire strategy. Overwhelm and eviscerate from the inside out. So, let's reiterate. A fact-finding mission once we get back to the stadium, then, as a last resort, Hans uses the Panzer armor to close up the fracture." Thornton powered down his datapad. "Now Mr. Cresher has a few words." He stepped down from the podium and took a seat next to Simmons, while Cresher jogged up to the podium and cleared his throat.

"Tomorrow, decades of planning and millions of dollars, yen, marks, wampum, whatever you want to call it, all comes together to form this group. This group of enhanced individuals has been brought together to make the most badass, dynamic bunch of heroes to take back the planet and look good doing it." Cresher slammed his fist on the podium. Arthur rolled his eyes. "We need to show the world what you are all capable of. If we can convince the world we can save it, maybe we can get more help out here."

"You do know this is a suicide mission, right?" Walker grunted from the back of the room. "Chances are we aren't coming back. Doesn't matter what you want to show people. Unless it's our dead bodies on the front page of every remaining newspaper, I don't think you're going to get much."

"He's right," Mia agreed. "I'm not sure this is even a good plan. Bring us together only to split us up? I don't see the point."

Cresher's features darkened. "Fine, you want me to get real with you? Here it is. You're probably going to die, and then all our efforts go down the drain. You think you're the first team we've thrown at them like this? We've tried almost everything else and nothing has worked. Do you think that's the proper mindset to take into the field of battle? No! Frankly, this is our last shot before the remnants of the US Government decide to drop nukes into every fracture on the planet." Walker flinched.

"This is our reality, and this is what we need to do. That thing," He pointed at Arthur, "needs to be front and center of all of it. We are monitoring and recording every aspect of this operation in any way we can, so we can get funding and more assets to use in the field. Since satellite and GPS uplink are a no go, every piece of equipment we give you is recording," Arthur felt a little violated. The rest of the crew all glanced at their equipment. Hans kept his attention and his grin on his face. "Do your jobs, stay alive, and maybe we can get help for the next mission. You're dismissed." He huffed his way out of the meeting area.

Dr. Simmons motioned for Arthur, Thornton, and Hans to follow him to the lab. Once there, he brought the team over to where the lab technicians were working on some new equipment.

Arthur was still uneasy from the briefing. *How much information were they getting from him?*

Did they have access to his memories? Wait, what did he say about a first team? If they did have access how much contro-

"This way, gentlemen." Simmons tapped on his datapad. Arthur snapped out of it. A locker opened up and revealed two armored gauntlets. He motioned for Thornton to come over. "We took your gauntlets and made a few modifications based on designs from Mr. Schreiber's equipment."

Thornton picked up one of the gauntlets. The glossy black shined in the lab's fluorescent lighting. "It's a little heavier."

"Yes, it is, but as you can see there is no power pack. They can individually deliver their own charge, up to fifty thousand volts." Simmons beamed with some pride. "Go ahead, try them on."

Thornton removed his trench coat and slid the gauntlets onto his hands. Then he pulled a small cable from them and plugged them into the back of his head in ports that Arthur hadn't noticed until then. He unraveled the whips to the floor and gave them a few slings before retracting them. "This will do. Thank you, Doctor."

"Don't mention it. We also have some armor for you in the other room if you wish to try it on."

"That's all right. I need my range of motion to stay the way it is right now."

"Very well. Arthur, for you, we have something special here. Take a look." Simmons tapped open another locker. This time a small piece of metal slid out on a silver platform. Simmons removed it from the platform and handed it to Arthur.

"Cool. What is this thing?" Arthur asked.

"It is the next piece of the puzzle for you. When we unlock your full potential, this will help your head and your mind stay together when times get tough. Here, let me put it on." Simmons motioned for Arthur to turn around. When he did so, Simmons clipped the device to his neck.

The metallic piece expanded around Arthur's head. All but the face of the helmet was the same multilayered alloy as the rest of his armor. The top of the face was a curved glass piece from ear to ear.

"Neat. What all can this do?"

"It's a reader. It can scan and give you readouts of lots of things out in the field. It works a lot like Dr. Thornton's glasses here." Hans and Arthur looked at Thornton, who didn't flinch.

"What? I do a lot of research. I need calculations... and sometimes everyone's vitals," he answered, despite there being no actual pressure for him to do so.

Arthur frowned. "Yeah, okay, man. We believe you." He deactivated his visor. He almost felt dirty for having it.

The last thing Simmons wanted to show them was in the next room. "I heard what Mr.

Walker said about the idea that this is a suicide mission. It really doesn't have to be. I have here a possible solution to our problem." He opened the hatch to the next room. On a lab table were six packets with straps attached. "What we have here are the first phases of what's called the Fulton recovery system."

Arthur interrupted. "Yeah, you guys kept mentioning that. What even is that?"

Simmons happily answered. "Normally, on an operation these packets would inflate. The weather balloon would take the cargo or personnel up into the sky for recovery via passing aircraft. If you are stuck inside the fracture, though, you can use the Fulton, make your way out of the fracture, and release when you get to the top. Simple, right?"

Arthur picked up one of the packets and inspected it. "So we make our escape by hot air balloon? Sweet."

"Essentially, yes. They should be capable of carrying more than one of you in case the unspeakable happens."

"Very good, Doctor. We appreciate you doing everything you can to help us survive." Hans laughed and gave the doctor a big hug. "We are off to prepare. See you all on the drop ship tomorrow."

"See you, Hans. Let's go, Arthur, we've got some recalibrating to do." Thornton pulled out his datapad and left the lab. Arthur put the Fulton packet back on the table, shook Simmons' hand, and left with Thornton.

After a few hours, in which the crew ate lunch, prayed, or in Walker's case, took a nap, the Xtremis operatives met in the staging area.

Walker was at his own station cleaning his weapons. His Barrett M107 sniper rifle, several types of handguns, a pair of MP5s, and multiple stacks of grenades lined the table.

Hans was loaded into the bottom half of his armor, lying on a bench, lifting what looked like 350 pounds with relative ease.

The Sakurais were reattaching their armor to their bodysuits. Mia had her hair done up in a bun again, while Yoko let hers down before sharpening her wrist blades.. Arthur noticed that most of the scorch marks on Yoko's armor set had been cleaned off.

Thornton was at his own station running diagnostic tests on his new whip gauntlets. Arthur watched him while a team of scientists replaced parts of his own armor. Dr. Simmons came up to him, tapping on a datapad.

"Are you ready for this?" he asked.

"As ready as I'm gonna be, Doc. There's nothing that can stop us. This is a great group you guys pulled together. The last line of mankind and all," Arthur responded.

"That's good. I'll tell Cresher to use that in his reports."

Arthur grinned, and the scientists finished by clipping his katana and the helmet to his armor.

He got off of the table, retracted his helmet, and flexed, making sure his entire range of motion was within his capabilities. Everything seemed to be all right and ready for combat.

"Oh, one more thing, Arthur." Simmons waved over another team of scientists. They carried with them an armored leg, not unlike the pair of legs he already had. "Which hand is your shooting hand?"

"Oh, uh, right hand, I guess."

"Great, have a seat. You can look away if it weirds you out, but we need to switch this out."

"Oh." Arthur shuddered. "Yeah, just make it quick." He looked away while the scientists switched out his right thigh. Arthur tried wiggling his toe as it was detached from him and to his grisly dismay, it moved. When he was told they were one hundred percent finished, Arthur looked down and saw that the new thigh looked just like his previous one. "What was the point of that?"

"Stand up for a second," Simmons said with a smile. "You know how you asked me about a RoboCop leg? Well..."

"Are you serious? Wow, you guys are fast." Arthur hopped onto his right leg. It felt just the same as his previous one.

"Here, let me prime it so you can control it however you like." Simmons punched a few buttons on his datapad, and Arthur felt something jolt in his body.

"Oh, oh, that's good. Here we go." Arthur clicked open the side of his leg. It opened up, exposing a holster with a fully loaded Desert Eagle inside. Arthur grabbed it and looked at the weapon. It had XTRE-MIS engraved on the side in a logo embossed in an American flag. The weapon's heft conveyed the damage it could do to a smaller Demon, maybe a Gamma. He tried not to get choked up. "This is the coolest gift you guys have given me. Besides, you know, my life back."

"Think nothing of it, Arthur," Simmons said. "This is just another step in making you the best. We need you to bring this group of talented, enhanced individuals together. It's mankind's last line of defense."

"You guys keep saying that, and I find it hard to believe."

"If the world can't come together to fight this common enemy, then humanity as a whole is done for. Sure, some countries will last a little longer thanks to people like the Sakurais and Hans, but without any help, those countries will eventually fall. I genuinely feel that if this operation fails, we're done." Simmons stared off into the distance, perhaps remembering what the world had gone through in the last twenty years.

Arthur looked at Dr. Simmons and his thousand-yard stare. The Desert Eagle in his hand felt heavier, and he decided to put it away. He spun it around on his finger before sliding it into his new leg holster. The holster closed up around it, keeping it ready for action.

"Don't worry, Doc. I won't let you down."

THE CALM

At close to 3 a.m., Arthur still laid awake in his bunk. He couldn't sleep, mainly because of the noises regularly heard on an aircraft carrier—fire drills, aircraft landings—and a crippling fear of what might happen if he went back to sleep. Would he wake up somewhere else again? How much control over his own body was actually his? How much of it does Cresher control? His blood ran cold. He glanced over at Thornton with whom he was rooming and saw that he was fast asleep. Arthur was grateful that they were given an officer's quarters, and out of the whole group, he was happy to be rooming with Thornton. Even so, with sleep eluding him, he decided to get up and explore the ship for a while.

As he made his way through the passageways, he would pass a sailor or two and stop to talk with them. In doing so, he got to know more about the ship and how it ended up being home base for the Xtremis program. Apparently, the *Reagan* was close to being decommissioned as more advanced nuclear carriers were being developed, but the Fracture changed everything. The *Reagan* had been used as the largest civilian evacuation runner, taking refugees from California up to Alaska. Only recently had the ship been reassigned to patrolling the Pacific waters. It had definitely seen some action and along one particular bulkhead there was a running tab of demons killed. The etches into the metal symbolized how hard it was for conventional weaponry to kill them. One particular sailor brought up that normal military shock and awe tactics were useless against the Demons because they didn't seem to show any kind of fear.

After Arthur asked, the sailor explained that normal shock and awe tactics were the backbone of the military's power for most of the twentieth century. A bomb goes off and it has such power that it is terrifying to an enemy soldier. It was the core concept behind the victory in world war two. The nukes were so powerful Japan surrendered immediately. That stuff didn't work against the guerilla warfare tactics used by the Viet Cong in Vietnam, and it didn't work against the beasts that were annihilating humanity. It made Arthur's stomach sink. Everything Thornton had told him about how bad things had gotten was true. He felt like every person's story piled onto one another making a massive mountain of death and despair.

Arthur eventually found his way into the laboratory where Dr. Simmons was awake and working on several monitors.

"Ah, Arthur! Is that you? How are you, my boy?" Simmons said with a smile as he looked up from his work.

"I'm okay, Doc. I've been having trouble sleeping."

"Totally understandable. It's hard to determine the side effects of the process. Come, sit down."

Arthur trudged over. "Okay, since we have a moment. I just want to talk to you about... I don't know. All of this?"

"Okay, where would you like for me to start?"

Arthur sat back in the office chair. He sighed and composed his thoughts. "Let me start with...why me? Why did you take me and not someone else, someone who had kids, someone who was a doctor or something?" He started to tear up. The guilt was eating at him from the inside.

"Well, Arthur, it's a combination of needing someone with your abilities and sheer luck," Dr. Simmons answered. "When we started the program, it was originally to design the soldier of the future, so our research largely focused on enhancing the brain's existing abilities. Then we expanded into augmentations for missing limbs, such as for veterans that were injured in the line of duty. Since you were highly trained in many forms of martial arts, you were on a short list of candidates."

"What happened to me? I only remember..." Lights flashed in Arthur's mind. Claws, demons, blood. "They attacked while I was on set. I remember something crashing down on me."

"We were keeping track of our candidates. We were lucky to find you when we did. We managed to get your body out of the rubble and into containment."

"What happened to the others? The others on the list?"

"They are still out there, the surviving ones. But unfortunately, all of our resources were diverted into making you the best we could. But it's not just about the technology. There is something about you that makes you special. Where the others perished in restoration process, you not only survived but you thrived! Every day you grew stronger and stronger and that is not something we did. That's all from inside you. We put all our hopes into making you an efficient killing machine because that's all we have left. Your best combined with our best!"

"But why?" Arthur wrinkled his forehead. "I saw the guns on this ship when they brought us aboard. We're not defenseless here. Why hasn't the military bombed the shit out of them?"

"If only it were so simple." Dr. Simmons continued, "Our bombs, missiles, and other artillery would be effective against human targets, but aren't effective at all against the Demons' biology. Fire bombs are ineffective, they emerge from fractures in the ground. Even if we physically blew up the crater exteriors, it wouldn't stop more from pouring out of the earth itself. The only thing that demons can do better than killing, is digging. Add on top of that the Beta's projectile defenses, and it makes for difficult operations from any trajectory."

"Beta?"

"Right, there's so many variations of Demons that we classified them by size. In Texas, we encountered the Gammas and that Iota, if you recall."

Arthur recalled his first time putting the katana to use. "Yeah, they were the size of, like, big- ass cats."

"And they only get bigger from there. The Betas discharge some… thing that prevents any airstrikes to penetrate into the fractures to try and close them up. Shells, artillery, missiles, bombs, nothing gets through. Not to mention the Deltas, the winged bastards." Arthur sighed. Simmons took notice. "I'm sorry that this is all so much to take in, but you are the key to this mission's success. As such, I think it is important that you know what we're up against. Try to get some rest, we've got a long day tomorrow."

Arthur got up from his seat and moved to the hatch used for the doorway. He looked back to Dr. Simmons. "One more question… 'Xtremis'? Why?"

Dr. Simmons looked up at Arthur. "Ah, yes. The project name was my idea. It stems from the Latin word *extremis*, which means 'at the point of death.' We dropped the E because it looks cooler." He grinned.

Arthur smiled and shook his head, muttering, "Buncha nerds," as he closed the hatch.

Arthur still wasn't settled. In fact, Dr. Simmons' explanations had made him feel far less settled, so he decided to go up to the flight deck.

He hoped the stars had at least stayed the same. Once he got topside, he was relieved to see that he could indeed see the stars. Outside of the carrier's running lights, the sky was free of light pollution and filled with a complete viewport of the galaxy. Arthur started walking toward the port side of the flight deck when he noticed a glow on the horizon beyond the control tower. Past the parked F-18s on the starboard half, beyond the fog that rolled over the ocean, a glow emanated in the distance. The fog was centralized off the starboard side near the land. Arthur saw that none of the other escort ships were anywhere close to it.

"The mist is from a fracture off the coast of San Diego. We're not very far from there," a voice next to Arthur said. He looked over and saw Mia sitting at the edge of the ship with her feet dangling over the side. She was wearing a T-shirt with a Japanese panda bear mascot that Arthur didn't recognize and a pair of fuzzy pajamas with some slippers. Arthur saw that she was still wearing the gloves from earlier. Mia kept her eyes on the glow in the distance. "It's where we're going."

"You're not cold out here?" Arthur said. He took a seat on the edge a few feet away from her. Then he remembered the fight earlier with her sister. "Do you not get cold?"

"Not really, but I just like to be comfy." Mia kicked her legs. "How about you? Do you get cold, Robo-San?"

He chuckled. "Robo-San, that's hilarious. No, I don't even know what I'm totally capable of feeling. Temperature so far hasn't been one of those things. I fought some of them, the Demons, in Texas with Thornton. I didn't even notice I was on fire at one point."

Mia laughed in return. "Seriously? That's funny." She finally made eye contact with Arthur.

Her blue eyes shone with a supernatural hue.

"Well, what's your story?" he asked. "I heard you saved Japan all by yourself. How does something like that even happen?"

Mia's gaze went from Arthur back out to the glow on the horizon. "It hasn't been easy," she said as the smile drifted off her face. "If I didn't have Yoko, I don't know if I would be alive."

"What happened?"

"The experiments that gave us these... *Maryoku*, these powers. Were very painful. I try not to talk about it."

"Well, why not? You don't think that you'll feel better letting it out?"

"Why talk about the pain from the past?" She removed one of her gloves. Her hand was solid ice, yet it moved like any other hand. Arthur couldn't keep his eyes off of the steam it made as the warm air got colder around it. "It has saved countless lives already," she said. "It must have been worth it, right?"

"I suppose it will be. But that pain is going to keep haunting you until you deal with it."

"Maybe, but maybe you should heed your own advice. Then maybe you could get some sleep." She stepped up off the edge of the deck and smiled at Arthur. "It's going to be a long day tomorrow. It's our first mission as a team, and I would hate to be embarrassed because our fearless leader was yawning out in the field. Good night."

CHAPTER 10

INTO THE MIST

The Xtremis field operatives had geared up and were walking across the hangar to the elevator. Walker did a final count on explosives before handing a sack full of them to both Arthur and Thornton.

"Here, take these."

"What for?" Arthur checked the bag. There were at least half a dozen grenades he didn't recognize in it.

"These might just save your life. A little batch of my own recipe for fun." Walker grinned. Hans noticed it was the first time he had actually seen him smile, which made him even more concerned.

"What's the casualty radius for these?" Thornton counted his grenades as well.

"The idea is that it's enough to make a mountain fall in on itself, yeah? Measure it like that. Set 'em off, and get the fuck outta there. They're thermally insulated, so they won't go off fightin' these things until you pull the pin yourself."

"You got it, man." Arthur and Thornton strapped their packs on.

The elevator came to a halt, and its doors open. The transport vehicle, a UH-60 Black Hawk helicopter, was waiting for them just as the sun set over the Pacific Ocean. The group had determined it was safer to go at nighttime for cover. Besides, the Demons couldn't hide in the dark, making them easier targets.

Cresher was wearing fatigues and combat boots, a stark contrast from his usual wardrobe.

His earpiece was attached to a combat vest with more pockets and zippers than he actually knew what to do with. He and Dr. Simmons were already strapped into the chopper and waiting for the crew to arrive. They took their seats, strapped in, and the pilot lifted off of the aircraft carrier.

"Hey, can everybody hear me on coms?" Cresher spoke into his headset. Every field operative received a Fulton packet from Dr. Simmons while Cresher gave them a rundown of the plan again. "We're going to drop Team A, that's Morris, Schreiber, and Thornton, and Team B, the twins, off the south coast of Coronado. At that point, Team B is going to make their way across the bridge, securing it and clearing the way into the Gaslamp Quarter. Once you clear the path, the second wave will come in behind you.

"Team A, you will stay in Coronado and clear it of any hostiles, securing the loading area and making sure no demonic presence lingers. Walker is going to be riding shotgun here as we take back the Naval Air Station North Island, making sure there is no hostile activity on the rest of the island. Multiple choppers will be firing at once, but they are all decoys to make sure that Walker gets to put down as many Demons as he can hit. Once we section everything off, all teams will meet in front of the baseball stadium for the next step. Got it?"

"Yeah, can you repeat everything after the word, hey? I got distracted by your face and what I did to it." Arthur snickered to himself.

"I'll get you back soon. Dick."

"Yeah? You want to try it? Hang on, let me see here," Arthur patted around his body looking for something. "Ah, I found my anti-shitbird defense," His helmet clanked into place around his head, eliciting chuckles from the cabin.

"Go fuck yourself, Morris. Anybody else?"

Yoko raised her hand. "How soon will the second wave approach? There is a lot of ground to cover with just the two of us."

"As soon as Walker and the other choppers clear out the airfield we can start running soldiers and supplies in. Tactically, it's our best bet." Cresher sat back in his seat.

Hans looked at Mia, who nervously adjusted her equipment. "We will secure the island as quickly as possible. You do not need to worry. Help will be there when you need it."

Mia smiled warmly. "Thank you, Hans. I knew I could count on you."

Yoko whispered something in Japanese to her. "You don't have to humor them. We could take back the whole country by ourselves."

"What did she say?" Thornton asked, even though his glasses had already translated everything for him.

"Oh, she's just happy to have you all here as well," Mia covered for her sister. "Normally it's just us together with our backs to each other." The readout came across Arthur's visor as well.

He smirked at Thornton who gave him a slight nod in recognition. His smirk quickly left after he remembered all of this info was being recorded.

Thornton smiled. "That's good to know." He directed his attention to Walker, who had his eyes closed and the brim of his boonie hat pulled down over them. "Hey, Walker, you awake? I would like to let the group know if they can count on you or if you have a death wish."

"Apparently you do, asking me something like that," he responded with no change in his position.

"I just need to know if we can rely on you."

"You don't need to worry about me. I got Cresher here, and this cockroach can't die. It's win-win for me tonight."

Everyone but Cresher laughed. Walker's joke had undercut the tension they were all feeling.

Arthur couldn't shake that this might be the last quiet moment they spend together. Once the laugh died down, everyone stared at the floor, listening to the whirring of the helicopter's blades as it pushed into the fog.

Arthur turned and looked at Walker who still had his hat over his eyes. He slowly tipped his hat up and noticed the cyborg staring back at him.

"Don't you fuckin' look at me. You're all dead by sunrise," Walker said bluntly. Nobody wanted to admit they agreed with him.

WELCOME TO SAN DIEGO

Coronado, CA | 19:58

The helicopter found a spot near the southeast pier to drop off Teams A and B. It was a ruined suburb next to a pier where the wealthy once moored their speedboats and yachts.

Thornton waved the helicopter off as Arthur said goodbye to Dr. Simmons.

"Stay safe, Doc," Arthur said into his headset. "We need to keep upgrading me until I'm a walking tank."

"You're better than a tank, Arthur, and we've only begun to scratch the surface. Stay safe. I'll be monitoring your progress as we go. Remember! It's not about the technology, it's about what's inside you!" Simmons shouted over the helicopter blades' whirring. Arthur shot him a smile and a thumbs up as the chopper pulled away.

"Walker, report in every thirty minutes so we can keep tabs on one another. These coms aren't great but it's all we've got." Thornton said into his com while he adjusted his trench coat.

"Roger, that. See you at the baseball field," Walker acknowledged. The Black Hawk helicopter flew back out to sea to regroup with the other attack choppers. Mia waved goodbye to the helicopter while Yoko's wrist blades extended with a sharp metallic sound. The group steadied themselves in case the helicopter drew any attention. The unholy sounds of the Demons in the distance signaled the threats they had yet to face. Collectively, they breathed a sigh of relief when nothing came from out of the darkness.

"The bridge is to the northeast, we can sweep eastward to clear a path. Make sure no Demons surprise us when we get the twins out there," Thornton said.

"You got it. Which way are we going?" Arthur asked.

"This way," Hans replied. "If we get separated, know that the glow on in the distance is north. At least until the sun comes up."

"We should be at the baseball field by then. It's 20:00 right now, and we need to get to the bridge by midnight." Thornton motioned for everyone to move eastward.

At that moment, a screech pierced the air, forcing everyone to cover their ears as they scrambled to get into defensive positions. The proximity alarms were going off in Hans' helmet.

"Hans! How many?" Thornton shouted.

"A dozen, Iota class! They're moving as a pack!" Hans held his armored fists up, ready to fight. The Sakurais went back to back, keeping each other covered. Arthur stepped in front of Thornton and drew his katana, ready for battle.

"Stay behind me," Arthur whispered to Thornton. "I can handle it."

"Not your call."

The howls of the Iotas drew closer. "They are spreading out and circling!"

"Go, cut them off, we can't get trapped against the beach," Thornton ordered Arthur and pointed north.

Arthur took off as fast as he could toward the glowing light.

"More Iotas coming from the east. Get ready!" Hans stepped in front of the sisters and activated his shield generators. An electric current pulsed as the generator activated on his right forearm. He kneeled in front of them as the Iotas came at them in a sprint. The first two were repelled instantly and flew back in a lifeless pile. Mia took her staff and batted a Demon away from Han's right flank as Yoko came down with her wrist blades on another to his left. Hans punched a Demon away with his free hand. He then slipped behind another and suplexed it over his head, snapping the Demon's neck and crushing its spine.

Arthur ran towards the first group of Iotas. As he dashed, he split his katana in two. The pack of Iotas bore down on his position, the hyena-sized Demons howling and pouncing toward him. Arthur spun and sliced through the pack as if they were liquid. The Demons' blood sprayed and cooled as it hit the ground. The skirmish was over almost as fast as it started. Arthur cleaned his blades and reformed them into one before rejoining the others.

Thornton joined the fight as he punched and kicked several demons off the back of Hans' armor. Another Iota leapt towards Yoko. She was preoccupied, pulling her wrist blades out of a dead Demon, but the attacker was halted and slammed down out of the air by Thornton's whip. His gauntlet powered up and shocked the beast until it made a disgusting popping sound.

Thornton whipped the body away and cracked another Demon in the face with his boot.

Mia spun her staff around with expert precision, striking several Demons and slamming her staff down on another. Yoko tore through the creatures one by one, shredding them with her wrist blades, with no fear of reprisal from their dangerous blood. Hans grabbed two Iotas and smashed them together, breaking their bodies and throwing them into some rubble to the side. He brought his armored fists together and slammed them down onto another Iota, crushing its head.

The four of them took a moment to catch their breath; their brief respite from battle was interrupted by the orange glow of yet another pack of Iotas.

Hans slapped his helmet. "Last batch, hold the line!" he shouted.

"I've got it! Get behind me!" Mia exclaimed as she stepped in front of Hans. He activated both of his shields as he crossed his arms. Yoko and Thornton took refuge behind them.

Mia removed her gloves; the Iotas were closing in on the group. She slid her hands into the slots on her staff and charged it up. A pale blue light shone out of the glass at the end of the staff. The Iotas howled as they grew closer and closer. Mia slammed the staff into the ground as a blue pulse-wave froze the speeding Demons in their tracks directly in front of their little group. She released a sigh of relief as she put her gloves back on.

Hans dropped his shields, the fight was over.

Thornton adjusted his gauntlets and looked around. "Arthur?" he yelled. The only response was a deep howl approaching.

"Shit, incoming Gamma!"

The group formed up again, anticipating that the threat could come from any direction. "Signal incoming, east side!" Hans shouted.

The Gamma was smashing through the frozen Iotas. A loud whistle rang out. "Hans! Heads up!!"

Arthur was running at full speed opposite the Gamma. Hans turned around and reflexively ducked to one knee. The Gamma drew closer. Arthur leapt in the air directly on to Hans.

He bounded off of the bulky set of armor straight up into the air, as high and as hard as he could. Arthur came down directly on the Gamma's head with his katana pointed directly downward, impaling its head into the ground. He stepped on the Gamma's head to get some leverage to pull his katana out. The death rattle of the Gamma made Arthur flinch, but he cleaned off the katana before replacing it in its sheath.

Thornton retracted his whips. "Report."

"Nothing on my scanners," Hans reported. He shot a glance at Arthur for such a risky maneuver. "For now."

"We're clear," Mia chimed in after Yoko nodded to her.

"I'm good." Arthur walked over to Hans and tapped his armor a few times. "That was fantastic. Great job, Hans." Arthur was thoroughly impressed at how efficient everyone was working together. For a field test with no training this was going exceptionally well. Which only worried Arthur just a little bit in the back of his head.

"We're not out of the woods yet," Thornton warned. "Let's get moving."

"What's the next step?" Mia asked.

"We head east to Orange Avenue. Then follow it north, checking your corners and making sure nothing gets behind us. When we get to the bridge, we can check in with Walker." Thornton made another equipment check to make sure all of his grenades were intact.

Suddenly everyone was thrown to the ground as the earth shook with fearsome power. "What's happening!?" Arthur yelled.

"It's another fracture," Thornton responded while trying to keep his balance. "It's gotta be close by!"

The group held together, trying to stay afoot. Almost as fast as it began, the quake had subsided.

"I hate those," Yoko spat out in Japanese.

They could hear explosion after explosion coming from the west.

"Must be Walker and the rest, taking the airfield," Hans said as he pulled himself to his feet.

"Walker, come in. Walker!" Thornton shouted into his headset. There was no response except for garbled static. "Has to be some interference from the fracture that just happened. I'll keep trying to reach him."

"Wait a second. Is that—?" Arthur trailed off as he wandered toward a burned-out building. "What is it, Arthur?" Mia called to him, but he didn't acknowledge her at all. He stopped in front of the remains of a burnt-out hotel. "It's the Hotel del Coronado."

"What is that? Is that a thing?" Yoko asked, retracting her wrist blades. "It's from an old movie. *Some Like It Hot*," Arthur answered.

Mia joined him in staring at the rubble. "I haven't seen that one. Were you in it?" She tried to be polite.

"No, no... it's from way before my time also. Marilyn Monroe, Jack Lemmon, one of cinema's all-time classic films. I thought it was hilarious, and I always wanted to come and visit where they shot it. I guess I'm a bit late for that." Arthur almost teared up at the thought.

"What's wrong?"

"I just... this is just some dumb place for people to relax and worry about nothing. A luxury hotel, completely superfluous and of no actual use to anyone. Humanity isn't on the brink of extinction because of the Demons. It's because we got soft. We had no way to defend ourselves because we were too busy trying to get laid or get rich... And I was just like all of them. Lazy and just trying to make as much money as fast as I could." Arthur's shaking was more out of anger than anything else now. "I want us to succeed. I want to help save the world, I really do.

We were never prepared for anything like this, and now the world looks like this." He gestured toward the rubble. "Shit we don't need is on fire while Mother Nature tries to take back the planet by purging it of its greatest threat." Arthur looked into Mia's brilliantly blue eyes.

"Us."

CHAPTER 12

ROADBLOCK

Moments earlier...

On the chopper, Walker adjusted his sights for the coming fight to retake the airfield. His bag of armaments lay ready beside him in case of emergency. Cresher and Dr. Simmons pulled up a holographic display of the airfield.

Cresher tapped on his headset. "Walker, we've got numerous bogeys on the ground. The other Black Hawks are the first wave while we circle the airfield picking off the big targets. Do your best to cover them. Also, let us know if you see any Ordinance Betas."

"Roger that," Walker grunted into the headset. The ten Black Hawks were flanked by a dozen Apache attack helicopters. Cresher hummed "Flight of the Valkyries" to himself as they approached the base, their pilot keeping a steady pace with the group.

On the beachhead, the light of dozens of Demons grew brighter and brighter. A pack of Iotas scrapped with a few Gammas on the ground below. They all stood fast in place when they heard the strange noises of attack helicopters coming through the mist. The Iotas howled and barked at the strange flying monsters coming directly towards them. Cresher's voice scratched onto the radio in every helicopter.

"Fire."

The front row of Apache helicopters opened fire with a hailstorm of bullets. The pack of Iotas screeched in pain as they were ripped to shreds by the large-caliber ammunition. The Gammas took several shots before succumbing to a similar fate. The howls of the dying Gammas reverberated through the cabin of the helicopter.

"Jesus, that's loud," Cresher said. "Heads up, more incoming. Pilot, take the flank!"

The pilot acknowledged and moved into their flank position as Walker opened the door and set up his rifle. A normal bullet would destroy a man, but the explosive-tipped bullets were worth their hefty price tag to Walker, mainly for their ability to take down a Gamma in a single shot.

The choppers continued their assault on the ground, opening fire on anything that gave light to the night sky. Rockets shot into pockets of Demons, spewing their hot insides everywhere, coating the buildings with flammable material. Collateral damage was not a concern for the strike group, just ruthless effectiveness and efficiency. A flock of flying Demons collided with one of the Apaches from the west.

Dr. Simmons shouted, "We have several Deltas coming in from the west side. We have to get them out of the sky now!"

"Pilot, take me over there!" Walker ordered. The pilot complied and rotated the helicopter so Walker could get a look. Several winged Demons ripped into two of the Apaches, tearing out the pilots and crew men. "Fuck. Keep it steady!" He aimed down his scope and fired off four shots. Four Demons fell lifelessly, heedlessly, to the ground. Proximity alarms blared on Simmons' display.

"Half a dozen more heading straight for us! Pilot! Reversal!" he commanded.

The pilot obliged, rotating the vehicle a hundred and eighty degrees so Walker could see. Six Delta-class Demons screeched and flared their golden wings as they dove straight for the helicopter. Walker fired off six rounds. The empty ammo clip clanged and rang out while the corpses of the Deltas crashed into the earth below. Two gigantic demons with large conical protrusions on their backs crawled out from underneath an airplane hangar. They charged up and spewed lava into the air around them, completely disabling several attack choppers.

"Betas! Right side!" Cresher marked them on the holographic display.

"On it!" Walker said. He took aim, but his scope itself wasn't close enough to see their weak point, the base of the neck. Walker's bionic eyes adjusted to zoom in enough for him to deliver an explosive round directly into their skulls. The Betas crumbled into each other as the unearthly glow bled from their wounds, their bodies cooling to rock.

"Take me to that rooftop there! Starboard side!" Walker shouted into the comlink.

A command tower for the airfield was still intact nearby; it would be a much more stable position to shoot from if he could get to the roof. The pilot lowered the helicopter enough for Walker to repel down to the roof with his equipment. "Get Cresher and the doctor back to the ship!"

The pilot gave a thumbs-up as the battle raged on around them. Just as he was dropped off a huge eruption in the center of the airfield threw Walker to the ground. "Oh, fuck me, not now," Walker said as he realized what was happening. A glow from the deep center of the earth emanated from a brand-new fracture, one that had just formed in the middle of everything going on in the skies above the airfield.

"Let's fucking go, pilot!" Cresher screamed.

An ungodly howl came from the new fracture. An aftershock caused the rooftop Walker was standing on to collapse. Walker made it a few feet before sliding into the wreckage that used to be a radio control tower. He grabbed his weapons and made his way around the rubble to a window. There he was able to see Simmons and Cresher's helicopter making its way back out to sea. But something followed them, something Walker didn't recognize. Walker had seen everything the Demons had to offer but this was beyond him. Standing eye to eye with some of the helicopters, nearly swatting them out of the sky. It must have crawled out of the new fracture to follow the VIP chopper. Walker used the butt end of his rifle to break the window and set up a shot, but it was too late. By the time he got his rifle ready, several brightly glowing tentacles shot out and grabbed ahold of the helicopter, keeping it in place while more tentacles reached into the helicopter itself.

"Dammit. I'm sorry, Doc," Walker grunted as he grabbed his equipment. On his way to find a new position to help the remaining helicopters, he didn't notice that he had dropped his earpiece when the roof caved in.

When he got to the other window he fired over and over, clearing out another Beta, a dozen more Deltas, and some of the remaining Gammas on the battlefield. The new monstrosity that had grabbed ahold of the VIP helicopter was nowhere to be seen. Walker saw that the fracture led all the way up to the command tower he was standing in, and formulated a plan.

"Right. Here we go then."

Walker packed up his rifle and brandished two polished sawed-off shotguns as he made his way back down to the ground floor. He kicked the door open to the first floor, weapons ready in case any surprises came to him or heard him working. He set his special-recipe grenades to go off on a remote detonation and began placing them in strategic locations on the first floor. Once that was done, he went outside. The heat from the new fracture was broiling the atmosphere around it. Walker had to put his oxygen mask on just to breathe.

He stood on one side of the fracture and used his advanced eyesight to do some calculations.

He looked up at the building and back down into the small ravine that had formed in front of him. His eyes darted back and forth until he found the proper positioning and throwing angle. In his hand he had the last ultra-special grenade that he made for the crew. He threw it at one particular spot in the canyon as he saw a new group of demons try to claw their way up towards him. Some of them leapt after the small, beeping, metallic object, but most ignored it.

Walker grabbed a shotgun in one hand and the detonator in the other, then blasted a Gamma that was getting too close for comfort. He hit the button and ran as fast as he could, even with all of the equipment he was carrying. The packets of explosives he set up in the command tower went off, and the eruption caused the building to fall on top of the fracture, clogging it up. He pushed the detonator again as he ran. The final bomb he threw into the fracture went up as well, collapsing the far side of the crevice inwards to itself, trapping the demons inside.

The airfield was quiet, with no signs of life from any helicopters or demons. Walker was alone, just as he liked it. He lit a cigarette and inhaled a lungful of that sweet nicotine he loved so much after a big fight, a chemical response he had come to see as both celebration and stress relief. He reloaded his weapon and looked down at the destruction he and the demons caused.

"That's for Simmons, you fucks. Dig your way out of that one." Walker spat on the ground, picked up his gear, and made his way to the rendezvous point.

CHINKS IN THE ARMOR

Teams A and B picked their way up Orange Avenue until they had almost reached the highway bridge that the sisters were supposed to take to the mainland. They took shelter in an old military base security gate before going the rest of the way. No Demons had bothered them up to this point, but they were concerned about Walker and the others.

"What happens if we don't hear from Walker once we drop the girls off?" asked Arthur. "We stick to the plan. Secure our point, they secure theirs. If we need to, we can split ourselves up to accommodate for their loss." Thornton relayed the plan as he adjusted his gauntlets. "The reinforcement wave is coming here at dawn regardless of what we do. We need to make sure the island is clear because if anything gets through, they're just going to be slaughtered."

Arthur sat in an old office chair. After checking himself for any damage and finding none save for a few scorch marks, he managed to let himself relax a moment. Their guard had been up for two hours moving across the suburban island. Normally it would have taken a person a half- hour to cover that same distance.

"It is a good sign that we didn't encounter any Demons on the way here, yes?" Hans said as he pulled off his helmet.

"Of course, but it's the explosions and radio silence I'm concerned about." Thornton grimaced. "I knew the airfield was going to be tough, but I thought Walker would be enough to secure it. This is my fault."

"Hey, don't worry. We can make sure the other soldiers won't have problems when they get here." Mia calmly placed her gloved hand on Thornton's shoulder. Yoko sharpened her wrist blades by scraping them together. "Come, we need to get going."

The Xtremis crew made it to the bridge, which stretched across the entirety of the bay and led directly to the old convention center. Arthur pointed at the bridge. "That thing looks like it's barely holding together. You sure you can make it over?"

"We can handle ourselves," Mia reassured him. Yoko nodded to her sister and took off running towards the bridge.

"Good luck, little flame! Burn well, and we will see the signal from anywhere on this earth!" shouted Hans as he waved goodbye.

"Very poetic, Hans. Good luck to you as well." Mia gave Arthur a hug. "Stay alive, you will see us again."

"Counting on it." Arthur's smile faded when he felt her cold body against his. He didn't even know he could feel anything so cold, much less a human body. Her brilliant blue eyes shone in the darkness of the night. Her smile was the warmest part of her entire being. "We're going to have to talk about ...that... whole thing going on with your body... when we get back."

"One day. I have to go. Yoko gets mad if she kills fewer Demons than I do. We have a competition going." Mia winked at Hans and Thornton before taking off after her twin sister.

Team A waved goodbye to their counterparts, not knowing what dangers awaited them. Their headsets scratched on, and a voice came on the line.

"Cresher? Is that you? Come in!" Thornton called into the microphone. The sounds distorted and warped until more sounds came through.

"Airfield... clear... -copter... Simmons—"

"What's he saying? The airfield is clear?" Arthur asked.

"Hold on, I can clean it up." Hans made some adjustments on his helmet display. "Airfield is clear, but the, oh my god." He gasped. "The VIP helicopter went down in battle. They have yet to find any survivors."

"Does that mean—?" But Arthur stopped himself. He knew exactly what it meant. Walker, Simmons, and Cresher were all dead. They had managed to secure the airfield but at a heavy price. "Shit."

Thornton pulled out his datapad and brought up a holographic map of the area. "There's not much time left. I suggest we take these routes to finish our sweep of the area." He pointed out three arrows on the map. "We come around back to the dockside over at this point. If we move fast clearing the island it won't be an issue."

"Splitting up? I mean, I'm sure Hans and I can handle ourselves..." Arthur began.

"Trust me, I've been alive this long, I can manage another hour. Meet at this point. I'll see you soon." Thornton headed west.

As Arthur watched his silhouette run off into the night, Hans slapped him a little too hard on the back. "I will take the south, see you in one hour!" Hans powered up and stomped back down the way they came.

Arthur was by himself. He thought about his last conversation with Simmons. Aside from Thornton, he had been one of the few who was there for Arthur from the start of all of this. He knew he still had a purpose, and that Simmons, Walker, and even Cresher had given their lives for humanity to regain a foothold.

He unsheathed his katana and took a back alley towards the southwest.

He knew that he could handle anything thrown his way, and he would live up to what Simmons had told him. He would be better than a tank. He would be unstoppable and take these Demons out by himself if he could. He had played the hero seeking vengeance before, but now he knew what it actually meant.

CHAPTER 14

KURIKO

Years ago...

Five-year-old Mia and Yoko Sakurai sat playing with some dolls in a lab somewhere deep underneath Tokyo. Mia smashed her two dolls together, while Yoko pretended hers was a baby. Their dark eyes occasionally panned to the mirrors surrounding them in the room. Though the girls couldn't know it, several unidentifiable figures wrote notes and observed them from behind the two-way glass. The lead figure spoke to the room via intercom.

"Good morning, girls. How are we feeling today?"

"Good morning, Father! I feel wonderful!" Yoko responded. Mia didn't look up from what she was doing.

The figure switched off the intercom and addressed the room of silent observers. "As you all can see, the girls have their particular personalities, which we are trying to use to augment their latent abilities."

One observer spoke up. "What do you wish to accomplish by experimenting on children?

Isn't that unethical?"

"What do we all want? To save the world. Within these two children are the latent abilities that we discovered in their genetic code that we can use to destroy the demonic plague. If our calculations are correct, they will manifest under extreme duress and we can then isolate it.

Replicate it. And arm the world's remaining armies with these abilities. If we happen to turn a profit at the same time, I don't see how that is so unethical." He shrugged.

The girls played in blissful ignorance of their surroundings, not knowing of their natural parents who signed them away before they were ever born. Or of the circumstances of the world beyond the walls they were so familiar with. Every male they saw was Father, every woman was Mother. They were all one big family. Their days were scheduled down to the half-hour. They could eat, sleep, use the bathroom, and play only at their designated times.

By age seven they began manifesting their abilities but only in small almost unnoticeable ways. Mia's ice cream would always take a little bit longer than Yoko's to melt. Neither of them ever asked for a jacket or a blanket, no matter how cold the laboratory got.

Once she reached nine years old, Mia grew restless.

"When can we go outside? We never get to go outside, Father!" she asked one of her handlers. The corporation never kept the staff that waited on them for too long, for fear of attachment, which may have altered the course of development for their powers.

Mia tugged at the metal collar on her neck. "Ugh! I hate you all! Take this thing off of me!

Off of both of us!"

"Mia, please." A voice rang out over the intercom. "What is our mission?"

Mia sighed as she looked over to her sister, who nodded to the speaker. "Our mission is to... save the world. Father..." She stared at the ground, clenching her fists. "But I don't have to do it for you!" She ran to the mirror and thrust her hands against it. She powered up and her hands became transparent with a blue hue like an icy diamond. A blue pulse-wave froze the mirror, so that when Yoko threw a small lamp at it, it shattered into a thousand pieces.

The silent observer took cover behind the desk as the girls helped each other out through the broken window.

"No! Wait! Don't go!" the observer cried to them.

The girls didn't stop. They didn't even stop when a pair of security guards came at them with batons. Mia grabbed one of the batons and cooled it down to an unbearable point with her powers. The security guard tried to drop the baton, but his hand was frozen to it. Yoko recognized the second guard as a smoker, and grabbed his lighter from his pocket. She flipped it on and huffed at the flame, expanding it and engulfing the man in flames. He fell to the ground to try and put himself out. Yoko held onto the lighter to use as a weapon if she needed to. She didn't glance back at the man who stopped screaming as they turned the corner.

Moving down one hallway, running down another, the labyrinth seemed endless to the girls. No alarms were blaring, no more security guards were in their way. They had no idea what to do when they escaped, but all they knew was that they would be fine if they stuck together.

Eventually, they came to a lone ladder well, labeled with the Japanese kanji for "Emergency". The girls tentatively looked around, but saw no one there.

"Go. I'll be right behind you," Yoko insisted.

"Okay." Mia tentatively started climbing. Yoko followed her up the covered ladder with the flip lighter ready in her hand. The higher they got, the slower Mia climbed.

"What's wrong? We're almost there! Keep going!"

"I just—Why aren't they trying to stop us? What's going on?" Mia knew something was wrong. They shouldn't just be able to leave. Was the company afraid of them? Had she and her sister killed those men earlier? Mia started to feel regret, and that maybe trying to leave wasn't such a good idea. "Maybe we shou—"

"Maybe you should keep going! There is a reason they kept us in here! Because if we tell everyone what happened to us they will go to jail! So go!" Yoko screamed at her sister. Mia was taken aback by this sudden outburst from someone who was normally so happy and so demure. She decided it was best to keep going and talk to her sister later.

Mia and Yoko made their way up to the top, where a latch was the only thing preventing them from reaching the surface. Mia pulled at it, but the latch was locked. She looked back at Yoko who gestured for Mia to use her hands again. She looked at the latch, which was metal and rusted. She had never tried something like this before with metal, and didn't know if it would work, but the last thing Mia wanted to do was let her sister down, especially after coming this far.

Mia took a breath, put her hands on the latch, and concentrated as hard as she could, pooling her energy into her hands. She felt her body trembling as she focused on the latch while struggling to keep her balance. Mia gave one final push as her hands became permanently like icicles. The blue pulse emitting from them transfigured the latch into ice, which, when pressured by Mia's weight, shattered and gave way. Mia fell from the ladder and was grabbed at the last moment by Yoko.

Yoko dangled from the ladder by her knees, barely holding on to her sister by the wrist. "Got you! You're a lucky one, huh? You wouldn't get anywhere without me."

Mia looked up at her sister and then down at the scraps of ice beneath her that used to be the latch. "What happened?"

"Your eyes!" Yoko saw in Mia's eyes that they had become a bright, icy blue. "They're so pretty!"

"Shut up!" she shot back. Then she shook her head, trying to regain her composure. "This was all your idea anyway!" She reached out to the ladder and regained her footing. Yoko sat up and continued up the ladder ahead of them.

Outside of the latch, on the surface, Yoko helped Mia up past the broken ice and the sisters stepped out into the world for the very first time. The girls were horrified by what they saw.

They were in the middle of a city street, but the buildings were bombed out and destroyed or on fire. Winged balls of light flew around the city, and other glowing monstrosities tore at the buildings and destroyed vehicles on the ground. The girls huddled together and cried in fear.

A pack of small Demons noticed the girls and, in a flash, bolted towards them. Mia and Yoko screamed as the Demons jumped at them. They covered their eyes, waiting for the flash of pain to come from the Demon's sharp teeth and claws. But the pain never came. The girls looked up only to see that the beasts were being held back by some invisible force. Repeated attempts to pounce at the girls were denied by an invisible force field. A loud thump refracted all around the girls every time a Demon touched it.

"Do you see now?" a voice rang out from behind them. A screen appeared on the force field, right in front of another pack of Demons tentatively clawing at them. It was the silent observer from before, his face half covered in shadow. "We didn't want you to see this until you were ready. But it seems you have pushed us to this point."

Yoko was enraged. "Why didn't you tell us?! YOU LIED TO US!"

"There was no way we could. I am sorry. Please come back inside and we will do our best to—"

"To what? To torture us again?! There is no such thing!" Yoko could not hold anything back if she tried. The Demons around them were getting incensed. Something within her was driving the beasts mad.

"The whole world isn't like this! We can work together to save it." The observer tried to speak some sense into Yoko, but she wasn't listening anymore.

Mia cried and hyperventilated as Yoko screamed. Her body was shaking with rage, and she slammed her hands together with force. Instantaneously, the Demons around them exploded, coating the force field with lava before it cooled into rock. Yoko fainted, but Mia broke her fall and caught her before she could be harmed. She looked at the monitor on the field.

"What just happened? Is she okay?" Mia's eyes shone, and tears of ice formed on her face. "Bring her back inside. I promise, I will explain everything and we will work together with you, with both of you, to give you the best chance at a normal life."

Mia held her sister tightly. Yoko started to awaken, her eyes had changed to a fiery red.

Blood dripped from her nose. "Wha... What happened?"

"Don't worry about it. You're okay. I've got you." Mia nodded to the monitor.

The observer sat back and breathed a sigh of relief. He turned and looked back at the conference room of investors from around the world. The monitor on the wall beamed security footage and replays of the escape attempt. Delegates, diplomats, and generals from various national powers, third world countries, and rebel factions looked on in amazement. One particular man in a German uniform was almost salivating.

"You see? Our girls displayed their true power once we gave them a little push. Limitless possibilities are out there for our methods. Maybe there is some hope for the world after all. All thanks to the Kuriko Corporation."

CHAPTER 15

TOLL

The Sakurai sisters, all grown up, continued their trek across the San Diego-Coronado Bridge. Mia kept a watchful eye on the mist around them as they leapt from cover to cover, avoiding any unneeded attention from passing Deltas overhead. Yoko kept her eyes forward, her wrist blades sharp and at the ready. They ran into a stray Gamma, which managed to slow them down more than they had hoped. Now, another obstacle was in the way, a twenty-foot gap in the bridge itself.

"How should we proceed?" Yoko looked back to Mia.

Mia thought about waiting for the guys, but they wouldn't get there in time. "If Hans were here, he could just throw us across," she joked.

Yoko held her head in her hands. "Remind me to punch Cresher and Thornton in the throat for not thinking of this." She looked around. Only a burned-out sedan and a toppled highway sign with lights were on their side. The side ahead of them was slightly higher with pieces of rebar jutting out.

"Hold on."

Yoko ran over to the highway sign. She looked over the gap at the other side and made some calculations in her head. "Pry this off. We need one panel."

Mia came over and used her staff to pry off the flat highway sign from the rest of the rigging. She helped Yoko drag it over to the burned-out vehicle. They placed it so that it bridge from the top of the car to the ground.

"You think this will work?" Mia asked her sister.

"When has anything I've come up with not worked?" Yoko replied confidently.

"I can give you a list when we get back to the ship." Mia smirked as she stood on the panel, knees bent and ready for whatever her twin could come up with. Yoko looked across the gap and moved Mia by her shoulders slightly to the right. She then took her spot atop the improvised platform and stabbed a hole into the sign. She retracted her blades and kept her wrist at the hole. A slight hissing noise could be heard coming out of the tubes on her arm.

Mia slowly realized what she was doing. "No—"

"Too late!" Yoko flicked her flame.

It expanded rapidly underneath the platform, sending the sign and the Sakurais careening across the gap. Mia kept her wits about her enough to grab ahold of one of the pieces of rebar. Yoko had a much higher arc and fell short of the gap. Mia's hand shot out and grabbed Yoko's before she fell into the mist below.

Yoko laughed. "Oh man, I owe you one."

"Yoko, you owe me nine. I'll remind you that this was also your idea."

"Whatever! Swing me that way!"

Mia scoffed. She swung Yoko back and forth a couple of times to get some momentum, before letting go of her sister. Yoko grabbed the next piece of rebar with both hands and, using her wrist blades, punched into the concrete and pulled herself up. Mia held tight with both hands, kicked her legs, and swung herself up to the ledge.

The ungodly howls of a pack of Demons penetrated the mist. Mia glanced at her sister. "Impressive, you managed to almost kill us *and* to attract unwanted attention."

Yoko sighed. "Damn. It's fine. This is fine."

A pack of Iotas and Gammas scratched and clawed their way towards them on the bridge, their glow enveloped and magnified in the misty night sky.

"It's fine, we can handle this," Yoko reassured herself more than her sister, and the two of them prepared for the incoming wave of beasts. Mia removed her gloves, revealing her icy blue hands as she focused her power. Yoko switched on her flamethrower, the small flicker burning at the ready end of her wrist contraption. She clashed her wrist blades together, hyping herself up for battle. "Come on, you bastards!"

Mia steadied her breathing. Keeping a level head always helped her in high stress situations.

The first batch of Iotas leapt at their prey. One was met with a swing of Mia's staff to the face. Another met a quick demise with Yoko's wrist blade jutting up through the jaw into its skull. Mia whipped her staff around, cracking another Demon's neck with a precise hit, and another careened off of the bridge.

"Home run!" Mia quipped.

Yoko sliced through one Demon's midsection while stabbing another that tried to jump at her head. She spun and retracted her blades, flinging the Demon's corpse into another Iota so that they both plummeted into the bridge gap behind them.

The Sakurai sisters danced a lethal and methodical dance, dicing and smashing their way through what felt like dozens of demons. The Iotas were dealt with, but that left three Gammas to confront. Yoko, incapable of sweating, manipulated the flame on her flamethrower and brought it into a fireball in her hands.

"You know they're not affected by fire," Mia shouted. "What are you doing?"

"My job." Yoko never broke her eyeline with the Demons. She swung her arms around and threw the fireball at a derelict car beside the Demons. The vehicle exploded and sent the Gammas plunging into the water below them. Yoko glared at her sister. "I told you, it's fine."

The bridge shook as bits of it started to crumble. Yoko had blown up a piece of the support column. The twins made eye contact.

"Run!" Mia screamed.

They sprinted as hard as their legs could carry them. Yoko blasted every obstacle that popped up in front of them: cars, downed highway signs, lamp posts, Demon carcasses.

"That's not helping!" Mia yelled.

"Shut up!" Yoko retorted as she kept running.

The two nearly made it to the end of the bridge before they lost their footing. The piece of road they were on cracked beneath them. Mia grabbed her sister with one hand, and in the other she used her staff to create an ice slide. They bounced off the top of the slide and slid to the safety of the shoreline in a heap.

As they lay there under the bridge, Mia looked up, checking for any danger. With relief she sighed and put her head back down.

Yoko retracted her wrist blades and made it to her feet. "I told you it was fine."

FOG OF WAR

Arthur walked along the burned-out suburb. He checked around corners and inside garages, making sure nothing would surprise the soldiers when they arrived in the morning. Most of the houses in the area were either affluent retirees enjoying the California sun for their retirement or military housing. Occasionally, Arthur would find remnants of people's lives that they left behind. A pile of bones in a kennel that was probably a family pet that was left behind. He saw looted mom and pop stores with windows blasted out and empty shelves. An exploded gas station that could have been either a Demon attack or a complete accident from a scared civilian.

He couldn't get the thought of Cresher, Walker, and Dr. Simmons crashing to their deaths out of his mind. Maybe the girls were right. Maybe they should have all stuck together.

Arthur shook it off. If anyone knew what they were doing it would be Thornton. He tried to not let the idea sink in that the number of his already limited friends was shrinking. Arthur pondered that if things didn't pan out, he could singlehandedly revitalize the entire film industry. He did his best to remember life before all of this. Growing up in the Midwest, leaving his house before he turned fifteen and running away to Hollywood.

He thought about what his sensei would say to him now.

You might be half robot now, but you are still too slow, boy! Arthur chuckled to himself as he threw a rock through what remained of a glass window. It reminded him of the alley his sensei found him in, stealing leftovers out of the dumpster. He kept his eye open for any Demon trouble while he took a break from walking to reflect. It was the most peace and quiet he's had since those first few days in that prison cell. Living out on his own might be nice, he thought. As long as the constant fear of death and dismemberment was dealt with.

Nothing was ever good enough for Sensei. Ultimately, his training did give Arthur everything he ever wanted. Money, fame, women. It all came to him fast. Almost too fast. He remembered got so wrapped up in the lifestyle he nearly lost it all when he nearly died attempting one of his own stunts. He drove a motorcycle in between two semi trucks and when trying to pull the wheelie he went too far and crashed into a production truck.

'My God,' he thought. 'I wouldn't even try that with this body.'

He thought about the arduous recovery process. His physicians, doctors, even his agent all came by to tell him that his martial arts and movie career were over. But Arthur pushed himself. He pushed his body to the limit in rehab, getting in even better shape than before the accident.

On days when he wasn't in the gym or at rehab he would study with private acting coaches, doing monologues, scene work, even cold reading for commercials. Anything he could do to get better, just in case something went awry with rehab.

His glorious return to entertainment wasn't even on film. It was on stage, landing himself a role in *Twelve Angry Men* and stealing the show. His film career was just starting to take off yet again with a role on a reboot of one of his films when—

Arthur sighed as he picked up a brick from a pile of rubble, he remembered the last day he was on set. That day he was signing a lot of paperwork with his new agent for some reason he couldn't recall. Ultimately, he felt it was probably unimportant in the grand scheme of things. Maybe there was some contest winner he had to sign autographs for or something. He didn't even hear the Demons breaking in. He just assumed some commotion was happening or some young grip was getting fired. He remembered seeing a Demon for the first time. The claws, the glow of the Demon's innards, the blood. What Thornton had called a Gamma, Arthur supposed.

He put the memory out of his mind for now and continued his trek through the suburb. No use crying over things he couldn't control.

Control.

Arthur activated his helmet. He tried looking to see if there was any configuration or settings he could look through to see what all he was capable of. A menu popped up on his HUD. After taking a moment to figure out how it all worked, he looked at an option marked DATREC and tried to open the file. A warning flashed on his screen:

ACCESS DENIED. PRIORITY 1 CLEARANCE REQUIRED

"Wait, how am I not priority one? I'm the guy running this." Arthur asked his helmet. The screen changed.

PROJECT XTREMIS MEMBER 1
MORRIS, ARTHUR: PRIORITY 3 ACCESS

He checked the other members of the team's profiles.

PROJECT XTREMIS MEMBER 2

THORNTON, CRAIG: PRIORITY 2 ACCESS

PROJECT XTREMIS MEMBER 3

SCHREIBER, HANS: PRIORITY 2 ACCESS

"Oh come on, Hans has higher priority than me?"

PROJECT XTREMIS MEMBER 4

SAKURAI, MIA: PRIORITY 4 ACCESS

PROJECT XTREMIS MEMBER 5

SAKURAI, YOKO: PRIORITY 4 ACCESS

"Awesome, we're running a misogynist and possibly racist program here. Fantastic."

PROJECT XTREMIS MEMBER 6

WALKER, BRAXTON: NO ACCESS

"Maybe that's for the best. Wait a second. What about–?"

PROJECT XTREMIS CIVILIAN MEMBER

SIMMONS, JEFFREY: PRIORITY 2 ACCESS

Arthur squinted at the last entry in his database.

PROJECT XTREMIS CIVILIAN MEMBER

CRESHER, PETER: PRIORITY 1 ACCESS

"Son of a bitch." The brick in his hand disintegrated into dust.

CHAPTER 17

CLEARING CORONADO

Arthur was fuming while wandering the suburbs of Coronado. Lost in his thoughts, Arthur nearly stumbled into a Demon he hadn't seen before. He ducked behind a garden wall to take a closer look. The Demon walked on all fours and was the size of a small horse, or perhaps a deer. It was chewing and gnawing at a garbage can hungrily. Arthur noticed it wasn't going after the discarded food or trash inside. It was chewing on the metal can itself, tearing it apart with a sharp and powerful beak. He took care not to make any sound as he got closer. The demon gnawed on a piece of metal it had ripped off and observed its surroundings. It froze in place when it saw Arthur standing there, unarmed.

He raised one hand slowly, holding out his palm. The creature tentatively moved towards him, dropping the bits of metal to the ground. It sniffed the air around Arthur's hand. The heat it radiated felt like the animal was a walking oven. Arthur hadn't been this close to a Demon that he wasn't trying to kill or vice versa. He knelt down to pick up a piece of the trash can that the creature was chewing on and held it out. The Demon sniffed at the piece of metal and snatched it out of Arthur's hand.

Arthur observed the creature up close while it gnawed at the metal. It wasn't like anything he had encountered outside of a nightmare. The skin was translucent and rubbery, and he could see the skeletal structure inside the creature. The Demon's feet had sharp claws where the bone protruded out of the rubbery skin. The tendons and muscle fibers connecting every bone glowed with the lava-hot Demon blood. Arthur felt that, scientifically, this monster shouldn't exist. It didn't make any sense to him. There was something supernatural about these beasts.

"Arthur!" A voice rang out from the misty shadows, and the demon took off running into the night. Thornton came through the fog with his whips extended and ready for a fight. "Thank goodness, I thought you were in trouble with a Demon."

"No trouble actually," Arthur said. "I think I just fed one."

"...What?"

"Yeah, it was really docile and curious. About the size of a donkey maybe?"

Thornton looked as though he felt both doubtful but that he should keep an open mind. "I didn't realize there might be peaceful demons out there. It's not in their nature normally."

"They don't seem natural at all. You ever see one up close? Their physiology doesn't make any sense."

Thornton pondered what Arthur had said. They had never caught one alive, much less been able to study one since they all cooled into rocks whenever one was killed. "I guess we just have never found anything out about them physically besides their ravenous nature and their hot blood with its magma properties."

"I think there's more to these demons than we realize," Arthur said.

Thornton retracted his whips and put a gauntleted hand on his shoulder. "You doing okay?

Anything malfunctioning?"

"No, I'm great. I can honestly say I've never felt better. Physically, anyway."

"I understand."

"You know, I'm not sure you do. One minute, I'm on set shooting a movie, then the next I'm writhing in pain because all my nerve endings are fused into a metal body. I'm still having trouble understanding everything that's going on. And now you're telling me that I just had the only peaceful interaction with one of them on record ever?" Arthur got in Thornton's face as he spoke.

Without blinking Thornton removed one of his gauntlets and held up his hand. Arthur couldn't help but gape. Tubes and plugs were spotted from his hand to down past his wrist. "We've all been through some shit. Believe me when I say I understand." Thornton loaded his gauntlet back on. "We through here?"

"Yeah, we're good."

"Good. Last thing I want to do is have you suddenly grow a conscience for these things because one didn't immediately try to eat you. They are not docile creatures, and they are not house pets. The best way for mankind to survive is if we exterminate them all or at the very least find a way to contain them."

Thornton headed north in a huff. Arthur felt a little guilty for going off on him as he followed the Brit up the road. They walked silently together, checking around buildings, clearing them on Thornton's map as they went.

As they came to an apartment plaza on the northern coast of the island, they heard metallic scratches and some bones crunching from the rooftop. The two exchanged a look, both of them fearing the worst before they ran towards the building. Arthur leapt up to a balcony and climbed up by jumping from balcony to balcony. Thornton watched until he was halfway up the side and decided to find the stairs.

As Arthur reached the rooftop, he saw Hans standing amongst a pile of Demon carcasses with a live one in his hands.

"Ah! Arthur! I see you made it up here! Hold on for one moment." Hans snapped the neck of the Iota in his grasp, then dropped its lifeless body onto the pile. "There we are. I'm glad you could make it! That was the last one in this building. We are all clear."

Arthur loosened his grip on his katana. "Great. Totally what I was expecting."

At that moment the door from the stairs slammed open. Thornton, sweaty from his climb, had his whips at the ready. He was just as surprised as Arthur and almost seemed disappointed that there wasn't any trouble. "Ah. I see everything is under control. Good to see you, Hans."

"Good doctor! Welcome!" Hans clapped his hands, clanging his armored gloves together. "It is good to see you both in good health. So, mission accomplished?"

"Objective accomplished, we've still got a long way to go." Thornton looked across the bay through the mist. "The stadium and the Gaslamp Quarter. Once we get those secured, we can hitch a ride back to the ship."

"Hold on a moment, Doctor." Hans picked something up on the scanner in his helmet. "It's the twins."

"What is it?" Arthur asked.

"They made it to the other side, thank god. The bridge did not survive their journey. And now we need a way across." Hans went to the edge of the rooftop to scan the area. The heads-up display in his helmet scanned some boats by the shoreline. "There. That one is still worthy of the sea."

"Which one?" Arthur looked over the side to see a half-sunk fishing boat. "You're kidding."

"Not kidding. It is the best option for you and the doctor."

"What about you?"

"I will be fine. I am too heavy for a boat anyway. I shall see you on the other side." With that, Hans leapt over the side to the ground. He landed in a crouch, and the impact of him and his armor left a small crater in the ground. He took off at a slow run. When he got to the water, the jets in his feet kicked on and he flew across, leaving a wake in his path.

His armor disappeared into the misty night, and Arthur and Thornton looked at each other. "Why is he so optimistic and nice?" Arthur asked Thornton. "I think I hate him."

"He grows on you."

"Yeah, and so does fungus," Arthur remarked as he leapt down from balcony to balcony, making his way to ground level. Thornton followed him using his whips to swing from a lamppost and smoothly land behind Arthur.

The two augmented men made their way over to the boat Hans had pointed out. Thornton grimaced as he grabbed the bag off of the side of a half-sunk fishing boat.

"This is a life raft." Thornton opened the bag. The bright neon of the life raft inside filled their field of view as it instantaneously inflated.

"There's no motor. What are we supposed to do? Paddle?" Arthur looked around them for anything they could use as an oar or perhaps a Remo.

Thornton waved him off. "Don't worry, I'm taking care of it. Get in."

Arthur cautiously piled into the life raft. Thornton retracted one whip back into its gauntlet, but left one whip out and put it in the water as he climbed aboard.

So that's his plan. "Oh, I gotta see this." Arthur took a seat near the prow. Thornton grabbed the support rope and sunk into his spot in the stern to balance it out. A small metal shaft jutted out of his gauntlet, and tiny metal clasps grabbed on to the whip. The whip began spinning, splashing water in and out, pushing the boat forward into the water.

"We should make land in front of the convention center. We can then make our way over to the Gaslamp Quarter to meet up with the girls and Hans." An explosion across the bay did nothing to assuage their fears.

CHAPTER 18

PANZER

Years ago...

Somewhere North of Berlin, Germany

Jonas Schreiber, a mountain of a man, was making some adjustments and modifications to the Panzer war suit he had designed for himself. His teenage son looked on through his welding goggles while he put the final touches on the shoulder-mounted cannon. The self-powered suit was his crowning achievement. Besides his son, it was the thing he was most proud of in this world.

"Father, this is incredible! I can't wait for you to test it out," Hans exclaimed. He beamed with pride at his father's creation.

Jonas lifted his protective face mask and smiled warmly at his son. His blonde bushy beard was covered in soot just like the rest of his pale skin, which was blackened from all of the smithing and welding work involved in developing the heavy Panzerschreck armor.

"My boy, we cannot idly strut about with this armor. We must be careful with who we can trust. We wouldn't want it to fall into the wrong hands, you know." He patted Hans on the back. "Do not worry, we will get the chance to try it out soon enough. We may even get to test out the Faraday countermeasures. Come, it is almost curfew."

The makeshift metal shop was set up in the barn not too far away from the farm that they lived and worked on, hidden away from the cruel world that was under siege from the Demonic threat that plagued the rest of the planet. Jonas did his best to keep his work and his son away from prying eyes and those who would exploit them. However, it was hard to acquire the materials necessary to build a technological marvel like his suit without stirring up any unwanted attention. Jonas locked the barn and tucked the necklace holding his key into his shirt-front. The rolling hills bounced the light of the sun so that the entire color spectrum was visible in the clear sky.

"Care to race? You won't beat me this time, Father!" Hans stretched mockingly.

"Well, I'm sorry. You know if I wasn't working all day I wouldn't be so tired that—" Jonas launched himself towards the house in a sprint.

Hans laughed and did his best to try and catch up.

The father-and-son duo laughed as they dashed down the dirt road alongside the wooden fence. They could hear the various animals on the farm squealing and munching as they sprinted by them all. The two really enjoyed the competition between each other. It was one of life's remaining pleasures since Hans' mother had passed away. Hans had grown into an impressive specimen himself, he could keep his father's pace while powerlifting with a superior intelligence and the grades to match, yet he always fell just short of what his father could do. Even so, he enjoyed the various challenges his father placed in front of them, whether they were mental or scientific or the occasional physical challenge. He had a knack for engineering just as his father did.

The pair rounded the pathway to their house when they both stopped in their tracks. Several cars were pulled up to the house, waiting for them to arrive.

"Who are they?" Hans asked.

"Trouble," Jonas answered, stone-faced. "Here, you know what to do." Jonas handed his son the key from his necklace.

"But, I don't..." Hans started.

"Hans, it will be okay. I'll see about making them go away for now. Until then, I need you to stay here. Only come to the house if I signal you, okay?" Jonas smiled at his son.

"Okay. But be careful," Hans warned his father. He gave him a long, concerned stare.

Jonas hugged his son in a big, burly squeeze that would injure a normal man. "No matter what happens, you will always be my proudest achievement," he whispered to his son as he let go. He walked towards the house, waving down the cars as Hans looked on and hid behind the nearby fence.

Moments later, Jonas was at the sink in the kitchen cleaning leftover dishes.

"If I had known company was coming, I would have cleaned up a bit better," Jonas joked to his guest, an older, uniformed man. "What was your name again, my friend?"

The man removed his uniform gloves and made himself comfortable in his seat. "You can just call me Rolfe, Herr Schreiber." He looked around the simple kitchen, observing the various handmade trinkets and displays. "You seem very talented, very gifted, Herr Schreiber. It's a pity the place lacks a woman's touch."

Jonas stopped washing the dish in his hands. He stared out the window where he could see the fenced area his son was supposed to be hiding. "My wife passed away many years ago. I haven't felt the need to do anything than care for my son since then."

"What exactly did she die from?"

Jonas paused. He silently remembered the monsters that had taken her, how he had to escape with their young son, how the country and certain wealthy parts of the world were now domed in with energy fields of his design to prevent any more death from tearing apart families like his.

"The Demons. Just like so many others."

"Ah. I apologize. It is a hard time for everyone. Except for you," the officer mused, "it seems, in your idyllic little life out here, protected by your work."

"I am not immune to what has happened out there."

"Then why do you condemn my wife to death?"

"Excuse me?" Jonas glared at the military officer. "What are you talking about?"

"Why do you condemn my wife, my sister, my children, and everyone else who remains alive to death if you insist on keeping the Panzer schematics to yourself!" Rolfe stood and screamed at Jonas. "We have made more than generous offers to you, and you still spit in our faces! There are forces at work across the world working to destroy not just our great nation but mankind as a whole! You should have seen these Japanese girls who had incredible powe-"

"I know what this government is about. You aren't trying to protect people. I've always tried to protect people." Jonas interrupted.

"Your shield designs are imperfect! They will fail eventually, and then what will the people have to defend them? Nothing, if you have your way!"

Jonas slammed his fist against the sink. "My shields are impenetrable! They will never fail.

You cannot lie to me about my own creations. You just want my armor so you can take advantage of the rest of the world in crisis. I will not allow that to happen. What good is taking over the world when it is nothing but ash?"

Rolfe was incensed. "I'm through with these games. Give me the plans or we will take them from you."

Jonas bellowed a hearty, defiant laugh. "You will never find th—" He was cut off abruptly by the thud of a bullet penetrating his chest.

The pistol in Rolfe's hand smoked as he reholstered it quickly. Jonas slumped to the kitchen floor, mouth agape as he gasped for air. Rolfe signaled at the cars, and half a dozen troops armed with rifles stormed into the farmhouse. They began tearing it apart looking for the plans.

Behind the fence, Hans looked on in terror. He looked down at the key his father handed him and clenched it tight in his fist. He sprinted back to the barn, as fast as his legs could take him.

He glanced around to make sure he was alone before he clicked open the lock with the key. After closing the barn door with the inside latch he took a second to compose himself. He was hyperventilating, but he knew he couldn't control the suit if he couldn't keep himself together.

Inside the farmhouse, Rolfe shouted at his soldiers. "Leave nothing intact, he's bound to have something here." The masked men toppled furniture and flipped tables left and right searching for anything hidden.

"Nothing yet, sir! Clearing the upstairs bedrooms now," a soldier with an extra chevron on his uniform reported.

"We will have to search the entire premises, stables, feed silo, everything. What can you... Wait. What is that sound?" Rolfe perked up at what sounded like a jet engine revving up outside the house.

Six uniformed officers turned to gape at what they saw out the farmhouse window.

The Panzerschrek Armor was floating clumsily outside the back door of the home. Hans had a difficult time keeping track of the various sensors and controls in his heads-up display but managed to steady himself for a tough landing. The massive metal boots clanged as they slammed into the ground. His breathing had finally calmed down now that he was in the protective suit his father created. He kept the over-sized shoulder cannon aimed into the house, directly at Rolfe.

"Well now, someone with some sense finally decided to turn their weapon over. It's more impressive than I could have ever imag-ined!" Rolfe kept his hands up as the suit approached. The spotlights from various points on the armor beamed into the house. Eight red blips appeared on Hans' display along with one faded blue one. Hans kept his arms crossed in a defensive stance and powered up the shield generators.

"Oh, it's the boy!" Rolfe crowed. "Well, I, for one, am happy you decided to forego your father's mistake and give up."

The armor stood silently while the red blips moved into position around him in a semicircle. Seeing through the walls with the use of his infrared scanner, Hans could see the pool of blood slowly expand-ing, cooling on the kitchen floor. His eyes filled with tears, and his lip trembled though he did his best to keep his composure. Everything he had in the world was gone.

Reluctantly, he lowered his arms and powered down the shields. The spotlights powered off, and the hum of the armor's energy slowed to a halt.

"That's good," the officer said. "Very good, my boy. Let's get you out of that thing and take you back to the base, yes?"

Hans spoke through the suit's speakers. "We're not... going anywhere." The words bellied the fear in his voice.

Without warning, the suit powered up and ran headfirst into the house, smashing walls and furniture as if they were made of toothpicks, making a beeline directly for Rolfe. The troops opened fire on the armor to no avail. The bullets bounced harmlessly away. Hans reached Rolfe, grabbed him by the throat, and lifted him into the air. He stared directly into Rolfe's eyes as he began choking the life out of him. Tears were streaming down his face.

"Switch to concussion rifles!" one of the soldiers shouted.

The others swapped their rifles out and began firing concentrated blasts at Hans. He felt every shot even though he was protected by the armor. The combined shots actually forced Hans to keep his balance. He responded by throwing Rolfe through the front door onto the front porch before sprinting at the closest pack of three soldiers.

He killed one of them instantly with an armored gauntlet to the face—the biggest fist Hans had ever made in his life. Hans somehow felt safer. He kicked the second soldier out of the back door of the house with a hefty boot to the chest, crushing his ribs and destroying any chance he had to breathe on his own again. Hans felt more relief. He grabbed the third soldier's head and flung him into two other soldiers, knocking them out cold. Hans wasn't crying anymore.

He powered up one arm's shield generator and spun into a huge backfist to the soldier who had just fired at him, sending him careening into a wall. The last soldier snuck up on Hans with a riot control baton and jammed it into the nape behind his neck before turning it on. The electric current had been redirected by the Faraday countermeasures his father had implemented, preventing any damage from such an attack. Hans slowly turned around to see the soldier standing there, unarmed and shaking. He knew he had made a fatal mistake. Before the soldier could run, Hand brought his hands together in a thunderous clap, crushing the man's head in between. Hans felt invincible.

Hans shook the bloodied bits of bone and gray matter off of the armor's gauntlets. He started looking for Rolfe only to be startled by the sound of a car starting up outside. He stomped his way out only to find Rolfe's body missing and a dust trail from one of the vehicles that had been parked out there.

He glowered. "You're not getting away that easily." Hans activated the rockets in his boots and legs and followed the dust trail down the road as level as he could.

Rolfe, in his panic, sped down the road in the military vehicle. He tugged at a shard of glass lodged in his temple until it released. He tried to hold his handkerchief to his skull to stop the bleeding while trying to drive with the other hand. The sun had set and the only light on the lonely German road shone from his headlamps. It was too late for him to react when Hans suddenly appeared in front of him on the road. The powered-up shield generators trounced the car. It skidded off of the road and came to a stop on its roof.

Steam and smoke billowed out of the undercarriage. Rolfe wasn't moving inside. Hans stomped his way over to the wreckage and ripped the driver's side door off. Rolfe groaned as Hans pulled him out by his foot and dropped him.

"How surprising to see... such a bloodlust... from you." Rolfe managed to wheeze out. It was proving difficult to talk with a collapsed lung. "Your father—ehk!" He was lifted by his throat off of the ground.

The steely gaze of the Panzer helmet leaned in close to Rolfe's face.

"You do not... get to talk... about him. Understand?" Hans gritted through his teeth. His heads-up display showed Rolfe's vitals dropping slowly while the life left his body. At the last second he let him go in a heap on the ground.

CHAPTER 19

GASLIGHTED

"I said it's fine!" Yoko shouted as she sliced an Iota to shreds.

The girls had made their way to the center of the Gaslamp Quarter before being ambushed by a swarm of Demons.

Mia spun her staff in a whirlwind of devastation, cracking her foes in the spine and neck, crushing their skulls with a well-timed plant into the ground. She crouched to a knee as Yoko ran towards her and pushed her up. Yoko twisted with both arms extended in a whirling dervish of blades and death, tearing several Iotas apart while their blood sprayed and cooled into rocks on to the walls and ground around them.

The ungodly howl of a pack of Gammas, at least half a dozen deep, came from down the street. They charged at the girls unencumbered as they battled the smaller pack.

"Okay, it might not be fine," Yoko said quietly. Mia heard her anyway. The pack closed in as the women slayed Demon after Demon. Both Mia and Yoko tried to not let panic set in as the enemy's numbers grew. They didn't know how much longer they could hold out. This is what they do, Mia thought. They overwhelm until we can't take it anymore. I have to keep trying. I have to keep her safe! I have to-

"HEADS UP!" a voice rang out.

Mia popped up to see the Panzer suit running toward them from the opposite end of the street. She ducked as Yoko kicked the last Iota towards the Gammas and sprawled on the ground to take cover. Hans charged up a blast from his massive shoulder cannon and fired into the oncoming herd of Gammas.

The Demons exploded in a glob of blood and bones that singed the area around them. Yoko blocked any from hitting Mia by standing with her arms spread wide open. The demon blood cooled into rock formations across her breastplate, which she brushed it off effortlessly.

Mia dusted herself off and thanked her sister with a nod, which she returned with a grin. She then looked over at their savior, Hans, who was stomping his way towards them.

"You made it!" she shouted.

"Ha ha! Of course! I wouldn't miss this for the world!" Hans kicked a Demon into the nearest building, powered up his shield generators, and plowed into the building after it. He grimaced as he made a mental note that the power level of his rail cannon was at sixty percent. Mia adjusted her pack of grenades before swinging her staff, catching an Iota in the head and flinging it harmlessly and lifelessly to the ground.

Yoko leapt off of a wrecked trolley and jammed her wrist blades into the neck of one of the remaining Gammas. It howled and ran, trying to buck her off, but it was too late. Yoko retracted one wrist blade and flipped underneath the charging Gamma, slicing it open from the underside. She shook off the hardening blood and sprinted back towards her sister.

Hans continued to plow through the base of the building, knocking over every support column he could see. The HUD in his helmet marked the load-bearing columns he needed to hit to bring the building down. Hans crossed his arms and ran at the closest one. The shield generators pulsed to life, expelling the column in every direction, turning it to dust. Hans never broke stride, leaning towards the next column and the next, blasting through them as if they were paper. Once he hit the last one, like a tree felled in the forest, the skyscraper began to crumble to its eastern side.

The Sakurai sisters were battling just outside as the building began to crumble. Hans burst through the wall in front of them.

"Get behind me!" he ordered. He spun around, protecting them from any falling debris as the skyscraper crashed down around them. When the dust cleared, they saw that the rubble from the fallen building had barricaded several city blocks, preventing any Demons from emerging from or traversing the rubble without being easily seen and picked off.

Mia coughed up some dust. "Phew, that's one down."

"One of too many. We have a lot more to go." Yoko cleaned her wrist blades in the glow of the fractures and the Demons.

"Above us!" Hans shouted as the alarms in his suit blared. "Pack of Deltas from the north!"

"I've got these," a familiar voice scratched on in his headset. Arthur leapt from a streetlight and ran horizontally up a nearby skyscraper with his katana drawn. His augmented legs pumped, magnetizing and demagnetizing so quickly that the girls were reminded of the hero from an anime they had watched growing up.

"You're still not getting enough height, your left hand has a grapple function!" Thornton instructed on the headset as he ran to join with the rest of the team.

"Of course it does," Arthur remarked to himself. As he ran to the edge of the skyscraper, he leapt away from the building and pointed his left hand out. Thornton pressed a button on his datapad, enabling the grapple function, and shot Arthur's hand at the pivot point. The hand punched through the concrete and used Arthur's momentum to swing up into the oncoming path of the flock of Deltas.

"Good god, that feels weird." Arthur retracted his hand, and as he encountered the Deltas, he swung his katana with ferocity and speed, decapitating one, two demons, clipping a wing off of another. "Three more left. Not enough time." Arthur removed the Desert Eagle from his leg holster and blasted away at the three remaining Demons. Their heads exploded as bullets sped through them and blasted out the opposite side.

Mia let out a gasp, watching it all unfold in the sky above them. Though she'd stayed still, Hans had wasted no time. He crashed out of another skyscraper's ground structure, causing it to fall in Arthur's direction. Arthur grappled over to the crumbling tower and ran alongside it, continuing his momentum for a leap into another pack of Delta-class Demons. He was on the way down when he realized he had mistimed his jump and leapt directly into the path of an oncoming Demon. The Demon dove directly into Arthur, snatching him with its front claws. Its beak gnawed on Arthur's forearm as he tried to pry it open with his free hand.

"AGH!" Arthur grunted as he struggled.

"What's happening up there?" Hans shouted into the microphone in his helmet.

"Hans, keep working on the barricade, but if you must know, a Delta has Arthur right now," Thornton answered on the coms.

"I can shoot it down," Hans suggested.

"Negative, your cannon would probably vaporize Arthur, too. Besides, we need you to keep taking down these buildings."

"But I can—"

"That's an order, Hans." Thornton cracked his whip, ripping an Iota off of Mia in one swift movement. "Yoko, I'm sorry but Arthur needs you now."

Yoko grunted in frustration. She squared herself towards the battle in the sky and brought her hands together, pointing them at the Demon that had Arthur in its grasp. The Demon loosened its jaw, and the beak that had his arm released.

"The hell?" Arthur said.

Yoko brought her fingers together and pulled them apart as if she was separating the teeth of a bear trap. The flying Delta continued to open its jaw until it went too far. With a sickening crack, it bent backwards, completely crushing the jaw, neck, and skull of the beast. The dead Demon still had a firm grasp on Arthur, but now was falling to the ground in a death spiral.

"What are you doing?!" Mia shouted at her sister.

"What? You don't trust me with your new boyfriend?" Yoko quipped sarcastically in Japanese.

Arthur started to panic. The Demon was dead but still not letting go as it plummeted toward the earth. "Little help here?!"

Yoko manipulated her hands, making the Demon turn over. At the last second, its lifeless body swooped into a horizontal trajectory and shielded Arthur as it skipped and ground to a halt in front of the group. Yoko collapsed in exhaustion as Mia ran to her side.

Arthur pushed the limp arms of the Demon off of him. He checked to make sure all of his parts were still intact and made his way toward the group.

"What was that?" he asked Thornton.

"You're alive, right?" Thornton replied without looking at him.

"Don't give me that. I thought we were supposed to be all on the same page. She can control them? Hans could vaporize me at any moment? You can control some of my motor functions?

What the hell is happening?" Arthur was livid. He shoved Thornton, who removed his glasses and got in his face.

"Back up!" he boomed forcefully. His aggression caught Arthur off guard. "If you had access to everything your body could do right away, your brain would physically melt! Don't put your fuckin' hands on me."

Arthur cooled off. "Fine. But what's the deal with the firebird over there?" He pointed over to Yoko who was being helped to her feet by her sister.

"She controls heated particles in the air, like the fire from her gear. Once things get to a certain degree, she can manipulate them," Thornton explained.

"It's not perfect, but in emergencies it's been a big help," Mia said. "It takes a lot out of her to do it."

"Oh, shut up," Yoko uttered to her sister. The thump of another skyscraper coming down caught their attention.

"Hans, report," Thornton barked into his comm.

"One more building to go, I'm inside now—hold on. There's something here..." Thornton's earpiece went silent.

"Hans? What is it?"

The Panzer suit of armor stood silently in the parking garage of the final building. The heads- up display showed Hans an anomaly on the scanners. "The temperature is rising in here, but I do not see anything. I will send you the readings now."

Once the information hit his datapad, Thornton took a deeper, intense tone. "Hans, I need you to regroup with the squad right now."

"One moment. Something's—oh, God." The coms went static with interference. The ground beneath them shook. Hans screamed on the intercom. "zz-ZZZ Kap—zzBzzzt I repeat we have a—BZZRRT—"

The Panzer armor blasted out of the building back towards the group. It fell into a lifeless heap blocks away. Yoko rushed over to check on Hans, while Mia, Thornton, and Arthur stood to face the incoming anomaly.

"What the hell is it?" Arthur looked at Thornton.

Thornton never broke his gaze from the building that was starting to crumble. A bright orange glow emanated from its rubble. An enormous Demon emerged, scorching the adjacent buildings and rubble, melting and setting trees ablaze with its touch.

"Ho-lee shit." Arthur gasped. "Thornton, you gotta cut me loose."

"I can't do that yet. You're not ready."

He turned to the man with steely determination in his eyes. "I can take it!"

"No, you actually can't. Physically you wouldn't survive."

"I'm willing to take that chance!"

"I'm not, and it's not your call!" Thornton extended his whips and powered them up. "We can take a Kappa Demon. We just have to be smart about it."

"He's not waking up!" Yoko shouted back to Mia.

"Get his helmet off! I can handle this," Mia ordered. She stepped up in front of the men and removed her gloves. The light coming from her hands glowed an icy blue. She grabbed her staff by the sockets and charged her energy. The tip of the staff shone brightly as it gained more and more power. Yoko located and unclipped the helmet's emergency release, which let out a loud hiss as she removed it.

The Kappa Demon stood on its hind legs. It rose up to its full verticality and roared, booming and shattering any remaining glass in the area. Two horns jutted out of its forehead and its massive claws cracked and strained as the Demon stretched to its full extension. It lurched towards the group, crushing everything in its path. It left pools of hot magma in its footprints.

"This one has to be at least three, maybe four stories tall..." Thornton analyzed everything he could as he looked around. His glasses displayed various probability numbers and scanned for methods of attack, but the odds in every case were astronomical.

Yoko pulled off the helmet. Hans was still alive, but unconscious. She tapped a few buttons inside his collar to make sure his vitals were okay.

"Well?" Arthur asked. The Demon marched closer. Mia continued to charge her staff, preparing for the worst.

A shot rang out in the night. The Demon halted in its track, and the group ran for cover, Yoko ducking behind the massive frame of the Panzer armor and shielding Hans' head with her body.

Three more shots. The Kappa stumbled backwards.

Another two shots perforated the giant and sent molten guts spewing out of every newly formed crevice in its body. It fell backwards in a heap of rubble. It let out one raspy howl before succumbing to its wounds.

The members of Xtremis slowly leaned out of their cover. The steaming barrel of a .50-caliber rifle was currently being used to ignite the red-banded cigarette that Braxton Walker preferred.

"Oi!" he said, after taking that first sweet puff. "You fucks don't know how to answer your radio?"

CHAPTER 20

MUKABA

Years ago...
Central Africa

"You hear? I'm not coming all the way out here for nothin'. Either you bring me to Mukaba now or I blow the whole place, understand?" Braxton Walker shouted at the villager standing before him. The elderly man didn't flinch as Walker blew a puff of smoke into his face. The pigment in his eyes were milky and discolored. Walker impatiently crossed his tattooed arms, staring daggers into the villager.

The villager seemed to be studying Walker's face. The way sparks of red splashed amongst the black stubble of his beard. The green of his eyes was brilliant, if bloodshot from his travels. "You may see Mukaba when Mukaba says. Mukaba says you see him if your eyes can pass the test," the villager told him.

"That's more like it." Walker spat on the ground. "What kind of test?"

"This way." The man brought him to a secluded area away from the village. There were several other villagers waiting there, armed to the teeth with assault rifles and other firearms. They were pointing their weapons at a group in the center of the clearing.

Walker tentatively made his way to the center group as the villager he spoke with politely nudged him with the muzzle of his rifle. The group consisted of what appeared to be two large Russian men, a silent black man playing with a knife, and some other men with Anglo-Saxon features of various ages and sizes. Some of them were talking quietly while others kept to themselves.

"Couldn't convince them either?" Walker quipped to the group. A short, balding man addressed him in a familiar New Zealand accent.

"Right, you came here for Mukaba, too? Heard about what he's doin' out 'ere, yeah? Me 'n' my partner Roddy came up and ran into these lovely people. I'm Filch." The short man extended his hand to Walker's.

Walker squinted at Filch's extended hand. Cautiously he shook it while keeping an eye on the other hand hidden behind the man's back. "Walker."

"No need to be jumpy. Yet." Filch turned around. "Roddy, I think the last one is here! We're about to get started!"

"What's goin' on? This test of his," Walker asked the short man as he walked away.

"No one knows," the black man spoke up. His gaze never left the knife he was playing with. "Yet we are all here for the same thing. Aren't we?" He stood up. His muscular build was at least a foot taller than Walker's as far as he could tell. "Tekka."

"Walker. And yeah, I guess we are. You think he can actually do it?"

"I have heard things. Nothing concrete, of course, but the reward is worth the journey, don't you think?"

"We'll see."

The villager that Walker had yelled at called for everyone's attention.

"Friends! Strangers! We all know why you are here!" his smoked voice rasped. "You have travelled far and wide to visit Mukaba and receive his blessings. However, there is only enough technology, time, and supplies for just one of you."

132

The group of men in the center of the clearing exchanged glances, simultaneously expressing worry while sizing each other up. Walker took note of who bunched up with whom and who separated themselves from the group.

The villager continued. "The last man standing, with the eyes of all the others, will receive Mukaba's blessing."

The group exclaimed in shock.

Filch shouted, "What are you on about? That's not what we came here f—" He was silenced as a large bowie knife penetrated his chest. He fell to his knees and collapsed on his side. The group stepped away from his body as his former partner Roddy began to cut out his eyes. After a squish and a crunch, the large man turned around to the group and held up Filch's bloody eyeballs.

"Like this?" he grunted.

Walker glanced over to the villager in charge. He nodded back to Roddy, who chuckled and readied his bloody knife.

Walker and Tekka both took off running into the jungle. The Russians grappled with Roddy and another hunter as things in the clearing broke down into sheer bedlam.

Walker leapt over a fallen tree trunk, his heart pounding as he scrambled to get away from everyone. He had to regroup and get his bearings before trying to do anything. He felt naked without his assault rifles.

Before he realized it, the night had crept up on him, and it had started to rain. Lightning crashed as Walker tried to orient himself with whatever landmarks he could see in the dark brush, cursing the fact that he had no time to prepare.

How the hell am I supposed to fight people off with no prep time? Who the hell does Mukaba think he is?

When I see that guy, I'm going to—

He was tackled into the mud.

Walker scrambled around and kicked off his opponent. It was one of the Russians, now by himself. In a flash, the Russian brandished a switchblade and thrust it towards Walker's midsection. Walker grabbed his attacker's wrist, spun around, and pulled the arm down at the elbow over his shoulder. A crunch and a scream rang out into the jungle air. The knife fell to the ground. Walker pivoted his body and flung the Russian over his head to the ground. Walker mounted the Russian and rained punches down on his face.

A figure crept up behind the scuffle, brandishing a similar switchblade to the first. Walker continued raining blows down on the Russian, unaware that his partner was sneaking up on them. The second Russian screamed that Walker couldn't recognize. The only thing he recognized was the immediate danger of a wooden stake hurtling towards him. He ducked out of the way in just enough time for the stake to fly over his head and hit the second Russian directly in the chest.

He looked up and saw Tekka creeping towards him from the brush, his knife at the ready. Walker snapped the neck of the Russian beneath him and readied himself for a fight. He rolled backwards and picked up the switchblade the second Russian had dropped.

The men sized each other up. Tekka was a bulky man yet deceptively quick. He seemed the type to be able to lift a small car but still nail a backflip confidently. Walker had what he liked to call "survival muscles." He had fought and scrapped his way through life, and in return, life gave him a chiseled physique.

They took a fighting stance, Walker bouncing with his bloodied fists up. When Tekka revealed yet another knife, he let out an exasperated sigh. "Oh, fuck me."

Tekka roared as he thrust the knife at Walker. Walker sidestepped the attempt and caught Tekka with a right hook to the jaw, jumbling his brain and forcing him to drop the knife to the ground. He followed with an elbow from the left side, disorienting Tekka even further. With his boot, he stomped directly on his opponent's ankle, crushing it, effectively ending their fight.

Tekka screamed as he fell over, grasping at his leg, the foot now dangling lifelessly in his hands.

Walker put his hands down. He wasn't happy to be forced into this situation, but he would be damned if he wasn't going to survive it.

"Sorry, mate. Business is business, right?" he said, not taking his eyes off of the dirt beneath him. His words escaped into the night sky as Tekka writhed in pain. No one was listening.

As Tekka began to crawl away, Walker picked up his knife. Calmly and coldly he kneeled down and slit the man's throat in a single movement. Walker waited in silence for the blood to drain out of Tekka's body before beginning to remove the eyeballs from the Russians. "Cor, this is fuckin' disgustin'. I don't get whoever the hell uses knives on purpose, ya know?" he said, to no one. "It's dirty, this kind of fightin'. Gets everywhere, you leave evidence everywhere, this shite is for the birds."

Back at the clearing, the villagers awaited any sign of survivors, and the village elder looked up into the night sky. While the trees provided much cover, the lack of air pollution this deep in the jungle brought the sky out like a bag of spilled diamonds on a black cloth. It was a much more pleasant sight than the death and gore of the trials that they set for Mukaba. The bodies of Roddy, Filch, and others littered the jungle floor, some with their eyes removed, others still intact.

The elder checked his pocket watch. He figured if anyone was still alive they would have returned already. He waved to the other villagers to begin piling up the bodies. "It's time. Once cleanup is done, spread the word that Mukaba is still looking for subjects."

"Cancel that!" Walker shouted from the trees. "He won't be needing any more sacrifices, will he?" He emerged from the shadows clutching a small sack in his hand, a whole bag full of trophies to prove his worthiness for this so-called gift from Mukaba. "Call off the search party, boys. I'm here to collect my prize."

The elder laughed. "You have done well, Braxton Walker! You have earned Mukaba's gift."

Walker threatened him with the blade. "Cut that third-person shite out, right, mate? I'll fuckin' add you to the crew here if this gift of yours doesn't pan out."

Mukaba smiled. "You are quite sharp, Mr. Walker. Have you considered the repercussions and... consequences of what you are about to experience?"

"You gotta tell me what it is first." Walker tossed the bag of eyes to Mukaba's feet. Mukaba's grin remained stuck on his face.

"Follow Mukaba, my boy."

The legendary leader waved him over to what seemed to be the largest building in the village. It was bolted securely and had power lines running into it from underground. Armed guards patrolled the rooftop and side entrances. Mukaba's guards opened a side passage for Walker and Mukaba to enter.

Once inside, Mukaba locked the hatch behind them and led the way into a grimy, dank workshop. "What is it you want, Mr. Walker? Why did you come out here?"

"I had heard rumors of what you were doing. I know about all the augmentation programs around the world. The Americans have theirs, the Japanese have theirs. Hell, even Germany has something going on with those barriers of theirs."

"And you have earned your right to be among them. We may not look like much, but we can give you what you want." Mukaba gestured toward a metal chair near some clean surgical tools.

Walker did a double take at the surgical tray. "Uh-huh, and how do I know you're giving me what I want, not just experimenting on me for your own freaky purposes?"

"I will show you." Mukaba opened the drawer of an inconspicuous toolbox and pulled out a chrome case. Walker moved towards him to see what was inside. Mukaba input the numerical code on the side of the case, and it beeped and hissed open. "You were already a master marksman, an asset to any military unit you were with. Now, you will be an asset to the whole planet."

Walker cracked a smile. Inside the case were two gray and blue eyeball-sized objects.

"This process will be absolutely painful," Mukaba said, "incredibly so. You must be sure this is what you want to do."

Walker remembered his wife and his daughter. He remembered their faces as he took off for one last mission. He remembered how far his heart had sunk when he got the news about Australia. If he would never see them with his own two eyes anyway, why not trade them out for an upgrade?

CHAPTER 21

EVAC

Walker's bionic eyes darted around the ruins of downtown San Diego. They didn't find any signs of life in the surrounding area. He hoisted his still smoking .50-cal rifle onto his shoulder and sauntered over to the rest of the Xtremis crew.

"Our radios are fine, dickhead!" Arthur shouted back to him. A goofy smile split his face as relief washed over him. Walker was alive.

Mia released the charge on her staff, and the glow from the tip faded away. She ran over to Yoko and Thornton, who had finally gotten Hans to sit up.

"*Mein Gott*, that hurt," Hans uttered. "What kind of Demon has such power?"

"Kappas are known to do that," Thornton replied. "If we found one, we're in the right spot.

The closer we get, the more intense the Demonic presence will be."

Arthur made it to Walker and reached his hand out. Walker glanced at it and handed him the bag of explosives. "Don't you pick up radio signals in your anus or something?"

Arthur's smile diminished to a sarcastic grin. "Yeah, but all I seem to get are smooth jazz channels. It's relaxing, but I have no idea what is going on." He held Walker's gaze as long as he could, hoping to get a reaction out of him but to no avail. Walker just stared right back at him.

"What? You don't like jazz?"

"No one likes jazz." Walker shook his head as the two made their way back to the rest of the group. "I'm surprised you're all alive."

"I was going to say the same thing about you. We heard the chopper went down. Are the others okay? What happened to Dr. Simmons?"

Walker hesitated for a moment, he kept his glowing eyes pointed at the ground. "I'm sorry, mate, I watched the chopper go down myself. There wasn't anything I could do."

Arthur sighed. "Well, we'll take any miracle we can get. I'm glad you made it."

"Me, too. What's up with the big bratwurst? He gonna be all right?"

"He's responsive, which is great. And he completed the objective, so we're evacuating now.

It's almost dawn," Thornton explained as he and the Sakurai sisters helped Hans to his feet. "We're not pushing on?" Arthur asked.

"Not yet. We've run low on power supplies for all of us, including you... probably. We've garnered a foothold on the mainland now, so the reinforcements should be coming through any moment."

"You sure the fire dogs won't be able to just burrow through?" Walker spat on the ground. "According to my calculations, they shouldn't be."

Thornton returned his glasses to his face. "Not to mention if they try to burrow through the tons of metal and concrete back there, the rest of it would collapse on top of them."

Arthur noticed Hans trying to shake the cobwebs out of his head. "Since we don't need medevac, you think we should just wait for the reinforcements to get here to hitch a ride back to the ship?"

Thornton nodded. "That's the plan for now. Mia, Yoko, Walker, you three establish a perimeter to make sure no stragglers are coming through. I'll run diagnostics on Hans and Arthur while we wait for our ride."

"Hai." Yoko nodded to Thornton as she took Mia and Walker to their positions along the debris.

Thornton watched them leave, then connected his datapad to a port on the neck of Hans' suit.

The numbers spread along Thornton's screen and matched up with what he had assumed. The suit's power levels were low and needed to resupply back on the ship. He turned his attention to Arthur, who had his eyes trained on the perimeter.

"You think this will hold?" Arthur asked.

"Of course not, but it will at least buy the military enough time to get dug in. Step over here a moment." He waved for Arthur to come closer. When he did, Thornton flipped open a port in Arthur's neck and stuck in a cable that ran to his datapad. Arthur shuddered at the feeling. It took a minute to boot up, but when it did, Thornton murmured, "Fascinating."

"What is it?"

"Your power cells are still over eighty percent. That's, that's actually unbelievable. I thought you would need to recharge but... you could keep fighting them nonstop for a week at this rate."

"Great. I'll clear my schedule then." Arthur pulled the cable out of his neck. "You okay, Hans?" In the short time he'd known the German, he had never seen Hans so shaken up.

"I'll be fine, my friend. The Kappa just caught me off guard." Hans shook his head and stood up. "But if he says we must go, then we must go. I trust this man with my life."

A thumping echoed in the distance. Thornton checked his watch just as Walker and the girls came back from their sweep. A wave of relief hit everyone when they saw the helicopter on the horizon. They survived. The operation, despite all odds, was a success.

Walker flicked his cigarette butt into the rubble. "That's our ride, boys and girls. The sun is about to rise, and we've got a distinct lack of bullets left!"

As the cigarette hit the ground, multiple APU transports pulled up behind them, dropped their ramps, and unloaded dozens of armored Marines, all shouting orders and directions. They spread out over the wreckage that the Xtremis team had wrought. The smoke and brimstone eventually was smothered out and gave way to sentry installations built with military and strategic efficiency. In the blink of an eye, the area was teeming with human activity.

One Marine with a captain's insignia on his helmet walked up to the team. "It's good to see you all! We got concerned when we lost contact with the helicopters!" He saluted and shook Thornton's gauntleted hand.

Arthur gave a return salute and smiled. "It's good to see you boys! You guys don't fuck around when it comes to working with your hands, huh?"

"That's right! Best of the best here with the Corps working with some Seabees! Every branch is pooling its resources these days. Your chopper will be here in a moment to take you back to the ship for resupply."

"Thank you, Captain. Xtremis, let's move!" Thornton waved his team toward the chopper flying in. Hans held his helmet under his arm, Walker slung his rifle over his shoulder, and the twins took one last glimpse at the surrounding area before moving towards their evac helicopter.

Arthur tapped Thornton's shoulder. "Hey, man, you know I could have taken that Kappa by myself if you had just let me hit 100%."

Thornton sighed to himself. "Maybe, maybe not. If Yoko hadn't grabbed you, who knows how that would have turned out, and I'm fairly sure she wants to kill you herself. She knows you are more valuable to the team alive than as another unmarked grave." Arthur looked away as he caught eyes with Yoko moving past him. "Walker could kill any one of us if he wanted. Walker gets it. Yoko gets it. Trust us, and then we can trust you. However, if I let you loose and your brain melted, I could never live with myself. You are too important to attempt this without more testing. And honestly, I probably wouldn't be alive at all because that goes one of two ways.

Your brain melts and so do the rest of your systems and then we die, or you lose your mind and everything that keeps you a good person, and you murder us all. Which would you prefer, eh?"

"I'd like to see him try to kill us. See how long he'll last, right? Hah!" Walker laughed as he climbed into the chopper.

"Hm." Thornton mused. "I'm pretty sure that's the only time I've ever seen him smile. Don't worry, though. When you're ready, you're ready. All right?" He slapped Arthur on the back with his gauntlet.

Arthur locked eyes with Mia who smiled back at him. He felt better knowing that they managed to survive all together. There was less pressure on him to be the ultimate weapon and keep everyone safe. Maybe the readings he got from their battle could get them some more support. He took a breath, put away his weapons and climbed into the chopper. The helicopter took off into the sky and turned out to sea.

The Xtremis team was tired and beaten, but not defeated. They all took in the sound of the helicopter blades and sat in silence, awash with relief. Arthur couldn't help but smile to himself. Mia noticed and began to smile herself. Arthur looked around the cabin. Thornton, smirked to himself as he tapped away at his datapad. Hans had that shit eating grin on his face yet again as he fiddled with bits of his suit. Even Yoko lost the constantly murderous look in her eye as she held her sister's hand. Before long the whole group was smiling, laughing, and feeling good about what they had just accomplished.

All that remained of the dilapidated bridge the girls had crossed was a few remaining support pillars, enveloped by the morning sunlight. Walker sat with a satisfied look as they passed over the naval air station where he reveled in the one-man war he waged against the demons.

But...

He leaned into the window trying to get a glimpse of Simmons and Cresher's helicopter. He remembered that it was pulled down into the crevice by the demon he couldn't recognize.

Perhaps if he could see the wreckage it would give him peace of mind, but he saw nothing, which bothered him even more. There weren't any helicopter parts or even any bodies.

Walker was certain he had left behind bodies—if not the pilot's then at least the Demonic rock formations. But they were all gone, too. The situation was just as dire as it ever was. The small victory they had won felt meaningless to him. Whatever smug look Walker had sported before was gone now. He slumped back into his seat, pulled the brim of his hat down over his face and muttered.

"Shit."

CHAPTER 22

SOLACE

A crew of lab assistants removed the upper half of Hans' armor. The helmet was on a nearby stand being analyzed for its combat data and recordings. Hans sat on a bench and downed a metal pint of beer in an instant. "Ah, set it over there and don't touch anything." He gulped.

Walker took all of this in from the workbench where he was cleaning his rifle. He made sure the bolt was locked open and made his way over to Hans. Walker glanced at the equipment being worked on, he stepped towards it when Hans slammed down the empty pint on the workbench in front of him. Clearly trying to divert his attention away from his gear.

"What was that?" he asked, nodding at the pint..

"Oh, this? This is my personal supply. It's hard to find any actual beer outside of Germany these days. You are free to help yourself. The keg is right over there." Hans gestured with his empty tankard and changed the subject. He never liked to admit he was very private with his equipment. Any misstep could ruin the precision he and his father put into it.

Walker declined the offer. "I've lost the taste for the stuff. I never liked German beers anyway. Too clean." Walker brandished a shiny silver flask and took a swig before offering it to Hans. He took one last glance at the equipment. "This, on the other hand, might help you grow out that shite excuse for a beard. Give it a try."

Hans laughed heartily. "I've tried some home brews in my time. This should be a walk in the park." He took a Hans-sized gulp of the drink and wiped his mouth with his sleeve. As soon as the liquid went down, Hans gagged and started heaving and hacking from the depths of his throat.

Walker grinned and snagged his flask back. "It's my own recipe."

"Ach! It feels like battery acid and Demon blood! What is that?!" Hans wheezed in between coughs.

Walker shrugged. "It's a little of column A and a little of column B." He slipped the flask back into his pocket and went back to his workbench, leaving Hans to scramble for some water.

Across the lab, Thornton glanced up from his datapad at the commotion before returning to his work. Arthur was sitting cross-legged on the gurney beside him, which was being used as a makeshift examination table. His eyes were closed, his hands clasped together. He was trying to meditate, despite the distractions.

"Is this something you normally do?" Thornton casually asked.

Arthur dropped his hands. One distraction too many. He kept his eyes closed as he responded, "Well, I haven't done it in decades if that's what you're getting at. I used to do this after a training session. It helped to chill me out and get my head on straight. My sensei taught me that it would do all this and help make me a better fighter."

"Uh-huh, so why did you go into movies instead of becoming a pro fighter?" Thornton asked.

Arthur hopped off of the gurney and stretched out his robotic legs. "I really didn't like getting hit in the face. Plus, I made way more money than I would have if I tried to be a prize fighter, you know? Not that money matters anymore."

"Yes, I suppose. It's not for everyone. And it does matter, for your information." Thornton checked the levels on his gauntlets, which were now charging on a separate workbench.

"That sounds like you have something to say." Arthur raised an eyebrow at Thornton. "Craig, did you used to hurt people for money?" he said sarcastically.

Thornton smirked. "How do you think I funded all of this equipment? I wasn't born rich, you know."

"I... guess that makes sense."

"I was a boxer. Underground, though. The Demons had already arrived by the time I was old enough to fight. Sporting events and boxing promotions sort of fell by the wayside. Not quite as important as making sure people weren't dying. I came up with the designs for these gauntlets, but I had no material, capital, or workspace to create them. But watching your movie, *Bull Fist*, gave me an idea to earn it. So, I went around crackin' skulls, making enough scratch to get my work off the ground."

"Oh, wow. I had no idea."

"I wouldn't expect you to, but I will say..." Thornton lowered his glasses. "You don't have to worry about getting hit in the face if you're any good."

Arthur looked at the smirk on Thornton's face. "You want a shot at the title, Apollo? I'll mop the floor with your mug!" he joked.

"Any time, old man." Thornton chuckled to himself.

The smirk left Arthur's face as he remembered something, "Hey, Thornton. I just remembered. I checked my files via my helmet. I assume there's information in here about what is and what isn't being recorded. But I don't have enough priority access clearance to get to it."

"That's weird. Are you sure?"

"Yeah, I found a file that says everyone's clearance levels and the only person allowed to look at it is... was... Cresher." Arthur detached his helmet and handed it to Thornton. "Is there something we can do about that? Since he's...you know."

"Hmm." Thornton looked at the helmet and took it from Arthur. He flipped it around trying to assess the technology. "There's a port on the back end here. Let me take a look at the files and see if I can't get administrative clearance to see it."

"That won't work for me."

"How do you mean?"

"I mean I need complete clearance to see everything going on in my head. How am I supposed to be in control if I don't know what I'm capable of?"

Thornton pondered for a moment. "Let me see what I have access to first and then we can have a conversation later about your limiters being removed. I don't even know if that will be possible without Cresher's authority. So, no promises."

Arthur nodded. It was the best he could hope for at the moment. The thought that Cresher may still have command over his body even after his death really bothered him.

Elsewhere on the ship, the Sakurai sisters were showering in the female berth. Steam rose from the extremely hot stream of water hitting Mia's face, while Yoko's shower was ice cold. Both of them were silent as they took in the moment of peace.

The two finished their shower and began dressing near their bunks. Like Arthur and Thornton, they had been given an officer's quarters, seeing as they were essential to the mission and there weren't many officers remaining to fulfill a large portion of orders on the ship.

The entire crew was a hodgepodge of Marines, soldiers, and sailors taken from whatever resources could spare them. The war against the Demons wore heavily on the military forces of the world, the United States' in particular.

The fact was not lost on or unnoticed by Mia, who found a picture of a little blonde girl with pigtails. She was holding a banner that read "Miss you, Daddy!" in glitter and finger paint. Mia pondered the fate of the man whose room she now occupied. She remembered everyone that she called father and mother, but still never knew who her actual parents were.

Yoko toweled off her short, black hair. She glanced over at her sister who was absorbed in thought. "I had everything under control, you know," she said, as she threw her towel onto their piled-up sets of armor.

Mia snapped out of it. "What?"

"When the Kappa attacked. But I'm glad to have you there in case I—in case I couldn't."

Mia frowned at her sister. "I know you could. But maybe it was for the best that Walker showed up when he did."

Yoko's lip pulled up into a snarl. "I wouldn't have been so worn out if it wasn't for your boyfriend. I had to save him from the Delta."

Mia's frown disappeared as her face blushed. "He is not... I-I'm not—He doesn't even—"

"It's okay." Her sister held up a hand. "He really proved himself tonight. He is very impressive. But just remember, the more you get attached, the worse it will be when they die. You know this."

Mia looked down at her penguin-themed pajamas. "I know."

Yoko looked up at her sister from her bed, which someone had told her was called a rack.

She could feel why it was called such a thing. It reminded her of the bunk bed they had at Kuriko.

"You don't have to worry about me, though," she said. "I don't think those things could beat me even if I tried to let them. But do you get what I am saying?"

Mia nodded "Yes, of course. It has happened so many times and the only permanent thing I have in life is you. I will never forget that."

"You better not! I have saved you just as many times as you have saved me. It's honestly too many times to keep track of. Whatever, it's fine." Yoko straightened out her phoenix adorned pajamas. "Try to get some sleep. We have more Demons to kill today." Yoko wished that she didn't have to say that every day.

CHAPTER 23

TKO

Years Ago...

Thornton Residence

A chubby, sweaty, boy is sitting at the window of his room, reading a book on basic electronics. A separate notepad was next to him opened and marked with notes, highlights and numbers.

Little sketches of animals lined the sides of the pages, more than a few were lions with names scribbled above them. Conroy, Kevin, Roger, Silas. The boy also had drawings of a strong man with a whip cracking and holding the lions at bay. It was all rather elaborate for a boy so focused on scientific studies. A bible sat untouched on the shelf among his other books. An Arthur Morris *Virtue Warrior* poster hung up on his wall. The matching doll (or action figure as it was pointedly marketed as) was posed in an elaborate display on his desk with the appropriate villains ready to battle. He was so intently focused on his reading that he hadn't noticed the black SUVs pulling up to the house.

"NO!" His mother shouted from downstairs. Her scream and sobbing pierced through Craig Thornton's concentration. Without hesitation he threw his books aside and shuffled down the stairs.

"Mum? What's going-," His rush to find her was cut short by the sight of several armed men in suits. The television was turned to a BBC news channel showing devastation in the United States all along California. The headline reading POSSIBLE TERRORIST ATTACK ON US WEST COAST. "What...who are these guys?"

"Come here!" Craig's mother opened her arms and grabbed him tightly. Her tears dripped on to his shirt as he squirmed to try and grasp what was happening. One of the suited men spoke up.

"Ma'am we have to leave. The primary requirement of the program is relocation to one of the SafePods. You and your son will be safe there while the situation is assessed." the man said.

Craig's mother took a second to gather herself, she gulped and took a breath. "I know." Craig was shocked.

"Mum, what? What are you talking about? What program?" Craig managed to get out before his eyes welled up. He knew everything was changing. He just needed something to hold on to.

"It's your father's job. They are here to help us. Some bad stuff is going on right now, and these men are going to take us to your father." She shot a glance over to the men and their weapons. They both looked at each other. Craig noticed one of them making a slight nod.

"That's right. We at the Kuriko Corporation are here to help. Your father was – "the suited man stumbled over his words. Craig stared. "... Is one of the greatest minds we have at the company. It is our duty to make sure he and his family are taken care of."

It wouldn't matter whatever the suited man was saying to him. Craig was long gone in his own mind. Wondering about his father, what was going to happen to him and his mother. What even are SafePods? He found himself standing in his room with his things and two empty luggage cases. This was all he had to take what was left of his life to the SafePod. He loaded up his clothes into one bag. The second he filled with as many books and notebooks as he could. All the materials he could find. He was going to get to the bottom of all this any way he could.

Whatever it took, if his father was in danger, he would be the one to rescue him. He didn't even look at his Arthur Morris toys in their meticulous display. In a matter of minutes, he was packed and ready to go. Almost on queue his mother yelled from downstairs, "Craig, it's time!"

"Coming Mum!" He picked up his bags and shuffled out the door. Stopped for just a moment, and reached back into his room and grabbed his Arthur Morris action figure.

Craig's mother was waiting with the agents downstairs who were loading her luggage and some other boxes full of files into the car. She hugged Craig after handing his bags to one of the men. As she held him close, she said to him, "Baby. Don't you worry, we have each other and everything is going to be okay."

But then she leaned in very close and whispered to him. "Do not trust any of these men.

When we get the chance we are leaving as soon as we can, do you hear me? Do not trust them, or anybody else you see in a suit, do you understand baby? Do not trust any man in a suit."

Craig nodded his head and tentatively jumped into the car. What would be the longest car ride of Craig's life was permeated with a sense of dread and unease. His mother never taking her eyes off the men driving them. He would never forget what his mother said to him that day. Not after her death when they escaped. Not after he heard his father was dead. Not after he was alone in the streets of London. It's the mantra that kept him alive in times where a person would hope that those with could help out those without, but were found disappointed.

Do not trust any man in a suit.

CHAPTER 24

BRACE FOR SHOCK

Mia was awakened by the blaring klaxon that rang throughout the ship. As she sat up, she saw that Yoko was already piling on her gear, heading to the door. "Get up!" she shouted. "Something's happening!"

"What is it?"

"I don't know, but it doesn't sound goo–"

The room jolted to the side, sending the two sisters to the floor. The groan of metal tearing apart echoed throughout the passageways. Mia gathered herself together, quickly equipping her armor, grabbing her staff, and following her sister out of the hatch.

The chaos of sailors and soldiers moving to their battle stations was overwhelming. Panic and fear spread through the air as they scrambled to their designated positions. Most of them had never seen a Demon up close, and the ones who had knew that their odds of survival were minimal at best.

"This way!" Yoko shouted. She and Mia arrived at the mess hall on their level, pushing past panicking crewmembers. They couldn't believe their eyes. A Gamma-class Demon stood before them, gnawing at the remains of an unlucky sailor.

"Damn you!" Yoko cursed at the Demon. She leapt onto its back and dug her wrist blades into its neck, spilling its hot blood on to the cold floor. The monster writhed until it finished bleeding out. By the time the body got cold the sisters had made their way down the passageway.

The bulkhead creaked and groaned until it burst, spewing saltwater like a high pressure geyser. Mia focused her power into her staff and sent a blue pulse across the bulkhead, freezing the holes and sealing them, allowing the soggy crew to find an escape.

Arthur and Walker were firing away at the Demons piling into the hangar. Swarms of Iotas were coming in, tearing at anything metallic or fleshy. An F/18 in the hanger was shredded like an unlucky fish in a swarm of piranha. An explosion after a warhead was punctured sent Demon bodies flying.

Arthur shouted over to Walker, "I'm out!"

Walker fired off several rounds before lobbing two pistol magazines over to the cyborg. In one fluid motion Arthur ejected the empty magazine from his pistol, caught the new one in the pistol grip, slapped the end of the pistol to make sure it was secured, and began firing into the pack of Iotas near him.

One Iota slipped out from around a cargo box and leapt at Walker from behind him. Arthur tried to warn him, "Look out!" but before he could get the words out, Yoko sprinted and sliced the Demon in half. It fell into a lifeless pile of rocks on the hangar floor.

Mia slid next to Arthur, keeping an eye on his blind side. "Glad you could join us," he quipped, keeping his eye on his targets.

"What happened?!"

"I'm not sure. One minute I'm going over the next mission, and the next we get hit by something big. Hans and Thornton went down to the engine room to get it off the ship. Whatever it is, it let the Demons on board!"

Yoko and Mia took up defensive positions next to Arthur and Walker, making sure no Demons got past them.

Walker remembered the unknown Demon that grabbed his helicopter. He shouted over the gunfire, "We gotta get down there. I don't know what it is, but I've got a bad feeling about it."

"Which way is it?" Yoko shouted in English. "Every room looks the same!"

"This way, follow me!" Walker grabbed his rifle and slid around their cover towards a hatch on the starboard side of the ship. The rest of the team followed him, keeping a sense of their surroundings amidst the bedlam.

In the engine room, Thornton opened the hatch inside. Hans, missing his helmet, but armed with his own assault rifle followed him. "Mein Gott."

Almost an entire section of the bulkhead had been ripped off. In its place was a glowing tube, fleshy yet sharp where it was lodged into the steel. Seawater leaked in from the puncture points. Thornton kicked one of them to get a reaction, but nothing moved. "So this is how they got on the ship. It's some kind of transport system I've never seen before."

"I thought the seas were safe," Hans said.

"They normally are. It must be because we're so close to the shoreline." Thornton shone a light into the gaping maw in front of him. "I don't know what this is, but we have to detach it."

"I have just the thing. Get inside and lock the hatch!" Hans ordered.

"I'm not leaving you in here alone with this. We've got enough problems as it is," Thornton protested. "Give me a second to figure it out."

"No time, the ship is taking on water. You have to see if there are any others onboard."

The water level in the engine room had already risen to their knees. "What are you going to do?"

Hans deployed a laser cutter from his wrist. "You need to go now. I have enough power left in my suit to get me up to the surface, but I can't take any additional weight. You have to seal the door behind me." He disengaged it from his armor and handed it to Thornton. "Go!"

Tentatively, Thornton took the cutter. He locked eyes with Hans, silently agreeing that he knew what he was doing and what his suit was capable of.

They both nodded, and Thornton slipped out the engine room hatch. A moment later sparks began spewing out around the seal of the hatch. Hans stood square with the large, gaping maw. His suit made him dwarf any normal man, but this glowing, toothed portal made him feel small. He put the rifle down, pounded his fists together, and took a deep breath. "What the hell are you?"

On the other side of the hatch, the rest of the Xtremis team arrived to find Thornton sealing Hans in.

"What's happening? What is it?" Arthur asked.

Thornton didn't look up from his work. "It's some kind of transport system. The demons used it to infiltrate the ship."

"Where is Hans?" Mia asked.

"He's inside. He's going to dislodge it from the engine room."

"Wait, what did it look like?" Walker asked.

Thornton continued sealing the door. "It looked like a large tube with teeth on the edges to clamp into the metal. Why?"

The memory of the battle at the airfield flooded Walker's thoughts. He remembered the tentacles that brought down the helicopter. It was that Demon, the one he didn't recognize. Had it followed them all the way out to sea? *Did we lead it back to the ship?*

"Get him out of there!" Walker shouted. "That might be the Demon that took down Cresher and Simmons. It's a trap!"

Hans clenched his gauntleted fists together and slammed them down on the clamped bottom teeth, crushing the bones underneath them. A pained howl echoed through the fleshy, glowing tube as more seawater poured in through the gap. Hans slammed his fist into one side of the gap, smashing it. Another pained groan came from inside the tunnel. Hans pounded the other side, destroying those clamps while yet another howl rang in his ears. Hans pulled a rebreather from his utility belt and stuck it in his mouth before reaching back to hit the maw one more time.

The clamps at the top of the gap released, and the Pacific Ocean flooded into the compartment. The tube retracted and closed up into a sharp point. The rush of seawater slammed Hans against the hatch and the sharp tentacle pulled him out into the murky water.

CHAPTER 25

FLESH & METAL

The Xtremis team could hear the compartment flooding. They could feel the impact of the ocean slamming into the hatch.

Arthur pushed everyone behind him. "Thornton, get everyone out to the next hatch! I'm going in after him."

"What?!" Mia cried.

"What are you doing?" Thornton asked.

"You're nuts, you know that?" Walker called, as he and Yoko were already running back to the second hatch. Water began spewing through the parts of the hatch Thornton had yet to seal, spraying the team that remained there.

"Agh!" Mia exclaimed as she put up an ice wall to block it.

"Hans doesn't have enough power left to take that thing on by himself," Thornton said. "Neither do you! We have to find another way!" Thornton grabbed Arthur's shoulder. Arthur pushed him back behind Mia.

Arthur kept his eye on the hatch. "I've got this! Mia! Keep the ship safe!" Thornton scowled as he knew he couldn't say or do anything to deter Arthur.

Mia and Thornton ran to the second hatch. Thornton clambered through, but Mia stopped and looked back at Arthur. Her icy blue eyes locked with his. "Be careful!" she demanded. Arthur nodded as she slammed the hatch shut. Sparks emanated from the cutter on the opposite side.

Arthur turned to face the hatch in front of him. He equipped his helmet with a rebreather and began prying open the hatch from its hinges. Soon enough the passageway was flooding.

The rush of air into the engine room took Arthur with it as he paddled his way in. He couldn't believe his eyes as he swam farther into the room, out into the sea. The murky water was permeated by an orange glow.

Hans was being thrashed about by a long, glowing tentacle. He pounded away at it, but his enhanced strength was no use underwater. Arthur unsheathed his katana and swam towards the struggle. He pushed closer and closer, trying to reach Hans. Hans continued his fight with the beast, straining to keep its razor-sharp end away from his face. The tentacle had wrapped itself around Hans over and over and began to squeeze the life out of him. Arthur knew his armor only had so much power remaining. He needed to break free to avoid a watery grave. Arthur finally made it to him and tried to pull the tentacles off, but they were too strong, even with his enhancements.

Arthur indicated to Hans he was going to cut the tentacle with his sword. Almost immediately the sharp end of the tentacle released Hans and slipped backwards in the water, backing away from Arthur as if it were scared of him. Arthur squinted through the murky water and readied his sword. He wanted to make sure this thing wasn't going to grab either of them. He swam towards it, but it disappeared into the orange glow, which also faded quickly into the depths.

Hans began to sink as his suit lost power; Arthur grabbed him by the arm and swam upward as fast and hard as he could for the surface. They didn't have much time left on their rebreathers, when Arthur felt something yank him back down into the water. He winced in pain as he looked down to see the tentacle hook around and into his leg. The claw dug into the leg that contained his holster, and the force of it pulling him down so rapidly it caused him to drop his katana. Hans reached out and managed to grasp it before it could fall to the bottom.

Arthur tried to forcibly remove the claw out from his leg, but the tentacle would not budge. He looked at Hans who was above him now, clearly trying to maintain his consciousness as his own rebreather began to lose its effect.

The remaining members of Xtremis peered over the edge of the flight deck, hoping to see if Arthur had been successful in retrieving Hans. Rain drenched the listing aircraft carrier.

Equipment, personnel, and several vehicles that were not secured tumbled into the sea below. Mia's heart sank when Walker indicated that there was no sign of either of them. "Something's wrong!"

Yoko could feel that something was down there with them. "It's bigger than the Kappa! I can try to move it away from the ship!"

"Don't! It might tear the ship apart if it's still attached! If we don't do something about that patch in the engine room, this boat is going down with it!" Thornton shouted.

Mia locked eyes with her sister as she equipped a rebreather. Yoko knew in an instant what she intended to do. "Don't!" she shouted.

Mia shook her head, and with a firm grasp on her staff and a running start, she dove off the edge of the flight deck, clearing the overboard safety nets with ease. She held her staff in front of her as she hit the water, freezing the molecules surrounding her and creating an ice tunnel as she continued to dive deep down below.

Mia burst through the end of her ice tunnel at full charge with her staff. She noticed Hans reaching downward to Arthur who was slowly being pulled into the depths. Mia pointed her staff at Arthur's trapped leg, and began freezing the sharpened tentacle that still latched onto it. The fleshy tube began to solidify until it became completely iced over. Arthur clasped both of his metal hands together and smashed the tentacle, shattering the end of it into pieces. Mia grabbed Hans by the hand and kept sinking towards Arthur. The tentacle shrieked and thrashed before retreating away from him.

Arthur lost track of it in the foggy water. *Whatever this demon was,* he thought, *it recognized me.*

He looked up at Hans and Mia and began his ascent. Mia turned towards the gaping hole in the ship, grabbed her staff, and swirled it in front of her, freezing the water in the engine room and plugging up the hole. Arthur grabbed Hans' other arm as he saw the icicles freeze over, effectively saving the ship from sinking. With one final movement, Mia formed a disc of ice underneath them all. It began floating up to the surface like a cork, carrying them up to safety.

Up on the flight deck, the other half of the Xtremis team looked down to the water, worried about their counterparts. Yoko paced back and forth impatiently until something caused her to lose her balance. She felt woozy and yet relieved. Walker steadied her so she could regain her composure.

"What is it, Yoko?" Thornton asked. "The Demon below. It is gone."

"They killed it?" Walker asked, hopeful. "No. It ran away, hurt."

Some sailors on watch nearby started making a commotion. "Hey! We've got people overboard!"

"Is it them?"

"Yeah, I think so. Not many cyber ninjas on an iceberg out here in San Diego. Call it in!"

Yoko smiled what Thornton believed to be the biggest smile she'd ever had. Sure enough, a frozen disc carried their missing teammates safely over the rocky waves. Thornton fell to his seat in relief and frustration. Arthur still wasn't following orders properly. Was it his programming or was it his ego?

Yoko sighed with relief when she saw Mia. Mia smiled up at her sister as Arthur waved up to the flight deck.

"Hey, you guuuuuys! Man, woman, and more attractive robot man overboard!"

Walker wasn't amused, he adjusted his hat back on and huffed inside to help with repairs.

CHAPTER 26

BACK TO PLAN A

Repairs on the U.S.S. *Ronald Reagan* were underway, sailors and other assorted crewmen working diligently to pump the seawater out of the engine room.

"Thanks to Miss Sakurai, we can have her up and running in a few days," Captain Tobin stated during the debriefing with the Xtremis team. "The sooner we get out of here the better. That was too close. We cannot lose another nuclear aircraft carrier in this fight."

"Hans and I will do what we can to expedite repairs," Thornton volunteered. Hans nodded in agreement; despite holding the ice pack to his head, he felt was mission-ready again.

"I appreciate that, gentlemen."

The officer looked ragged. Arthur surmised he hadn't slept in days. He couldn't imagine the immense pressure of being the commanding officer of one of the last battleships left on earth.

"Next item on the docket," Captain Tobin said, "arms inventory. We used a lot of our armaments in both the operation and defending the ship. We have enough resources to send one SEAL team with you when you take the stadium."

"Uh, how many troops is that? I'm not really a military guy," Arthur confessed. "That's all right, son. You will be assigned SEAL Team 12. They are stationed here in

Coronado and moved operations to the ship when the Fracture hit. A team consists of six platoons and one headquarters element, which will be stationed here on the ship. Unfortunately, we only have enough resources to pile together two platoons of sixteen men each. Leading the SEALs with you are Captains Joshua and McGahee. Gentlemen, come in here."

Tobin motioned to the back of the room. Two camouflaged officers, presumably Joshua and McGahee, walked in past the Xtremis team and took their places flanking the CO. A strong and fit Latino with dark hair and a prominent scar across the back of his neck was introduced as Joshua. McGahee was Caucasian, shorter and stockier than Joshua, but the gray hairs on his temples indicated that he was just as experienced in combat as his compatriot.

"Looking forward to working with all of you on the coming mission," Joshua said curtly.

McGahee nodded in agreement.

Tobin tapped his datapad, which brought up a holographic display of a soldier wearing advanced technology. Joshua pointed at various points on the display. "This is state-of-the-art, advanced wearable exo-suit, or AWES, technology. We have enough of these to supply our unit, which will give you all as much firepower as we can to take on the demons. AWES enhances the wearer's strength, speed, and lethality."

A gravelly voice spoke up from the back of the room. "You keep sayin' firepower. What kind of armaments do you have on these things that I'm not already carrying?" Walker spat on the floor.

Tobin grimaced as Joshua held his gaze. "Well, sir, each suit comes equipped with motion- tracking and infrared technology in the visor. It's not as advanced as your black-market eyeballs, but they can see

CHAPTER TWENTY-SIX

Demons well enough in the depths of the earth."

"Damn right they're not," Walker muttered to himself.

"Besides the standard M4A1 rifle, we have begun carrying the Harris compact wrist mount. It comes with a grappling cable and retractable spike, and each comes equipped with four rockets capable of bringing down entire buildings."

"Wow, have you used these before?" Arthur was impressed.

"We've done some field testing and training, but there aren't many of these to go around. It takes a huge physical and mental toll on the wearer. Of course, it varies operator to operator but those of us left are some of the best shooters out there." Joshua nodded to McGahee. Both men turned around and showed the group the backs of their necks. Two plugs stuck out at the base of each neck.

McGahee spoke up. "Yes, it hurts; no, you can't touch it. Any other questions?"

"They drill into your neck? That's terrible!" Mia exclaimed.

"It's no worse than what we went through." Yoko nudged her sister.

"Standard procedure with equipment like this. It's unfortunate that we don't have many of these units left, but we're making do with what we have, ma'am." Joshua turned his attention back to the display. "They also come equipped with jump boosters, allowing us to climb foreign terrain or slow a rapid descent."

"They turned you all into killing machines." Arthur smiled.

"No, sir, we've been killing machines ever since we graduated from BUD/S, sir," McGahee piped in. "And despite all of that, we're relying on you six to save the day."

Thornton stepped up to the podium and whipped out his data-pad. A small progress bar in the upper right-hand corner of the screen was nearly full. He glanced at the Sakurais and tapped a separate program, which opened up a holographic display of the Southern California region.

"Here we are." He pointed to a spot just southwest of San Diego. He then drew his finger back to the coast, leaving a digital trail that filled in with red. "We have taken back the island of Coronado and dug ourselves into the Gaslamp Quarter, here. We are going to continue the original plan to dive into the fracture at the baseball stadium, a indicated here." The display morphed into a 3-D view of the stadium and the earth underneath it.

"Why the stadium again?" Arthur asked.

"Valid question. This is the original fracture that hit San Diego. If we can get any readings from inside the fracture, we can assume they will be very similar to the original Fracture here on the San Andreas Fault. If we can find out anything about where these things are coming from, we can hopefully ascertain a way to stop them." The display zoomed out to show the rest of Southern California as a bright gold line thickened and divided the land mass. "Here is the original Fracture. The be-all and end-all mission is going to be to eliminate the source of these Demons and close this up. Unfortunately, it's become so massive and infested that nothing can get in there. If we can figure out a way in via the fracture here in San Diego, it may be the opening we need. What we're banking on is that they have a sort of hive like mind, bringing all of these fractures to a central point. If we can get to the origin, we may be able to put a stop to every demon straight from the top. The same way you obliterate a beehive when you remove the queen. We just need to know if there is a nasty queen bee to look for."

The room was silent. Only the low hum of the holographic display buzzed as everyone took in the gravity of their situation.

"It's a suicide run." Hans broke the silence with his low, gravelly voice. "Every run is a suicide run," Walker chimed in.

"No different from yesterday," Thornton acknowledged. "It's what we all signed up for."

"What? I didn't sign up for any of this." Arthur frowned.

"Actually, you did. I have a copy of your signature right here." Thornton tapped his datapad. What looked like a copy of some forms Arthur had signed: "To my biggest fan—Arthur Morris" appeared on the screen.

"I... how..."

"These are government forms, Arthur. You really need to read the fine print."

Arthur couldn't believe his eyes. *Yeah, that's my handwriting.* He lowered his glare to Thornton. "We need to have a talk."

"We do. However, this operation does not work without each of you committing to ensuring its success. You all know I'm in this for the long haul. We have the backing of the U.S. Government and the Navy SEALS."

"So I have a choice in this?" Walker asked. "Perfect. Toodle-oo." He got up and started to leave.

He made it to the doorway before Mia's staff blocked him off. The metal clanged against the bulkhead and resonated throughout the briefing room. Walker's augmented eyes met Mia's supernaturally blue ones. She smirked back at him and nodded towards the podium. He squinted at her before turning back around. "Of course, you all wouldn't make it ten meters down that hole without me. I'll take care of the entire lot o' ya."

Yoko silently retracted her wrist blades before she stood up. "Hai." She nodded to Thornton.

McGahee looked away when her fiery red eyes glanced in his direction.

"I'm relying on you guys," Arthur said. "We're all relying on you guys. We're all relying on each other. Let's make the world a better place. Something worth protecting... to the very end." Arthur stood up and fist-bumped Thornton. "Just as soon as you take these training wheels off."

Thornton frowned as he left him hanging. "We'll see. You didn't follow my orders back in Coronado. You've questioned me every step of the way. You didn't follow my orders when I told you not to go after Hans. Not to mention you got in my face when I had Yoko save your life. So tell me how I'm supposed to trust you when you won't trust me?" Arthur withdrew his fist and stood there stunned.

He dismissed the meeting, and everyone headed towards his or her assignments. Hans threw his ice pack into the trash and hurried out the hatch to get back to his equipment. Arthur caught up with Thornton just outside the briefing room.

"Hey man," he whispered, "I wanted to tell you—"

"No let me tell you somethin'!" Thornton interrupted. "I have been fighting these things for the better part of my life. You've been here less than a week! A weapon is useless unless you know how to properly aim it at the enemy!"

Walker stood around the corner and listened to their conversation quietly.

"Believe me when I say that I really want you to reach your full potential. But I can't do that if you're second guessing every order! We don't actually know how much of your programming is interfering with your emotions or your brain functionality! If we let you loose and then you lose everything that makes you human, then we're all dead! Do you understand me? You will.

Kill. Us. All."

Walker squinted at those words and left to go prepare. Arthur stood silently in the cold passageway. "You're...right."

Thornton raised an eyebrow. "Am I?"

"Yes, I...I'm sorry. I'm so used to being the top guy, you know? The star attraction. And then, all this happens and suddenly I'm the chosen one or something. I didn't ask for any of this but God help me, I'm trying to do my best here! I don't like that Cresher's people know my every move because some sensor in my bicep is telling them I've having a coffee. I don't like that mankind's ego and selfishness has driven us to the point of extinction. I don't like that in order for there to be any semblance of world peace or working together that we have to basically prove that it's worth the investment to save the world! I want to help but you are doing us no favors when you won't let me be the best... whatever I can be."

Thornton looked at Arthur, whose face was sincere and stern. Arthur continued. "Regardless of all of that. I gotta tell you something you might not have gotten from the others.

When we fought that thing, it seemed like it recognized me and tried to take me out specifically. Like, once it saw me, it stopped going after Hans. If Mia hadn't shown up, I don't know what would have happened. I don't know what that means, but these things don't have memories or anything like that, right? They're just monsters."

Thornton looked concerned by this new information. "They've never attacked us so far away from shore either. Something is...wrong." Thornton took off his glasses and rubbed his eyes. He suddenly felt tired. "Listen, I'm going to look into giving you some more freedoms if you agree to cooperate when the time comes. People die if we don't follow orders. Can we agree on that?"

Arthur felt a flood of relief. After needing so much backup, after being the weak link, he was grateful that he'd get the chance to hold his own. "I can. You won't regret it, man."

"I better not. Because as soon as you go rogue, I will have to put you down myself." Thornton looked away. "It's something I would rather not do."

CHAPTER 27

DIAMOND IN THE ROUGH

Arthur was pleasantly surprised to see that the outpost Xtremis had left behind was still standing. While plenty of rubble and debris remained, the makeshift operation base had been able to survive whatever had attacked the ship. Joshua, McGahee, and the SEALs flanked him, fully equipped in their exo-suits. Several of them threw glances towards Arthur. He pretended not to notice them.

Hans, fully armored, scanned the horizon. "Nothing to see here. No signs of the Demons."

"He's right," Walker piped up on their coms link. He was posted on the farthest wreckage of a building ahead of them. "There's nothing here, we're good to go."

"Ready up, team. Sensors are green across the board. We're moving out," Thornton commanded.

Yoko Sakurai popped her newly sharpened wrist blades as her sister made final checks to her fuel tank.

"Ready?" Mia asked her twin as she grabbed a couple of medkits from a tent for her pack. "More than you are."

Thornton checked his datapad one last time and waved Arthur over. The information on his touchscreen zoomed past as he ran the final diagnostic numbers on Arthur. "Arthur, I whipped this up before we left."

Arthur looked at the small device on Thornton's gauntlet. It was a metal cylinder with a red LED button. "Tell me this isn't the detonator to a secret bomb in my head."

"This one isn't," Thornton smirked. "But seriously, this Overdrive Trigger is the final stopgap to unlocking your full potential. I've made every software and hardware adjustment I could to prevent it from melting your brain when you activate it. I feel we can accomplish this mission without it. But, as you know, shit happens."

"Yeah, it does," Arthur remarked as he held the cylinder in his artificial hand. "Like to us."

"Especially to us. I'm going to hold on to it to save it as a last resort. Because when we're deep in it, the last thing I need is to put down a friend."

Thornton patted Arthur on the shoulder and jogged to catch up with the group. Walker watched from his perch as Thornton slipped the cylinder into his gauntlet. He made a mental note of where it was located and leapt down to regroup with the others.

"Little sister?" Yoko asked.

"Everyone knows I'm older than you," Mia corrected her. "By six minutes."

"Yes, but I can still bench more than you. Until that changes, you're little sister." Mia rolled her eyes.

"Anyway," Yoko nodded in Arthur's direction, "do you know what happens when he hits that button?"

"No, I don't," Mia confessed.

"Neither do I, and I don't like that. I'm not taking the risk, and you shouldn't either. I am the only one you can count on to watch your back in here. Can I count on you to do the same?"

Mia hesitated for only a moment. "Yes, I will do what I must to protect you. You are the only family I have left. You're the only family I've ever had."

The Xtremis team moved past the wreckage toward the baseball field. Walker moved along the sides, keeping his scope down the street in front of him. Hans took point with his shoulder- mounted cannon as the SEALs flanked the rest of the team. Joshua and McGahee's teams kept an eye on the side streets and alleyways, ensuring no surprises would hit their flanks.

They rounded a corner, and the baseball stadium was finally in sight. The enormous lighting fixtures were unlit and almost completely destroyed. The southern gate that they faced had split down the middle, exposing a warm, orange glow that seemed to get brighter the closer the team approached. At the gate, the team circled up as the SEALs took vantage points.

"Hold the line, gentlemen," Thornton said to Joshua.

"We'll do our part. We'll be watching for those balloons, Mr. Thornton," Joshua replied. He signaled for his men to spread out in their assigned positions.

The six augmented members of Xtremis started climbing their way down the crevasse that had split the south gate open. Arthur peered down into the crevasse and was certain that if he could feel vertigo it would have turned his insides out. It still bothered him that he didn't know exactly what percentage of himself was indeed himself. Climbing further into a dark cave was just as enveloping as the overall sense of dread surrounding the group. Arthur felt it was as if they were climbing down the throat of hell itself. The heat was starting to become a problem to half of the team. Yoko, Mia, and Hans had no issues but Walker, Thornton, and Arthur were sweating bullets as they made the journey further down. It did, however, give Arthur a small victory in his mind that he was still human. They only barely had escaped the enemies they faced before. Now they were all aware that they were climbing directly into Demon territory. Directly into the home of who knows what. Walker held on to his bag of explosives as tightly as he could. Hans punched holes into the rock face for his hands and feet as he descended, allowing everyone else to get a solid ladder to climb down. At some points the rocky face of the crevasse pulled together to make a tight fit for everyone to squeeze through. After some time, they came to a landing that allowed for no further progress.

"Guys?" Arthur pointed behind Hans to where the distinct, ominous glow came from. Before the team was an enlarged cavern that Thornton's glasses estimated to be twenty feet high and ten feet wide. An orange glow hinted at more demonic activity within.

"What do you think made this?" Mia asked, clutching her staff.

"I'm not sure, but if I had to guess, this is where that thing that attacked the ship came from. There have to be holes like this all over the globe. We've just never seen the bottom of a fracture before." Thornton assessed the structure. "This is where we put our charges to seal everything up. Walker."

Walker started placing some plastic explosives in sets around the side of the cave. "On it."

"This is our evac point, leave your Fulton systems here. Any excess equipment also, Walker.

I doubt you're going to need the rifle in these close quarters." Thornton motioned at his .50-cal. "You gotta be shittin' me. There is no way I'm leaving this here. This is high-quality equipment. You don't just go leaving it about, yeah?" He made eye contact with Arthur. "You wouldn't want the wrong people having such a powerful weapon, now would you?"

Arthur squinted at the Australian. He knew what he was trying to get at, but he let this one go. He had his own mind to worry about, much less what anybody else thought about the cylinder Thornton was carrying.

Hans took a long moment to disconnect his shoulder cannon and place it next to the pile of Fulton packs. Its sheer size would have prohibited him from moving any farther into the cave. The thought of moving on without being at a hundred percent would eat away at Hans. He tried his best to shake the thought away.

Thornton tapped the rail gun with his boot. "You know, Hans, I have some ideas that could help you make this a bit more portable. When we get back, I can show you."

"If we get back," Walker muttered to himself.

Hans shot him a look. He patted his rail gun as he left it behind. "That would be great, Craig.

Let's talk. Otherwise this trip might just be awkward silences, and nobody wants that."

CHAPTER 28

THE DESCENT

The team had been crawling for what seemed like miles. The rock walls closed in slowly as they made their path into the Demons' tunnel. However, there was never any doubt which direction to head as light always seemed to lead them closer and closer to danger. The heat was almost unbearable the further they climbed in. The rocks themselves were nearly scalding to the touch. The claustrophobic caverns made things difficult for Hans in particular to squeeze through. His armor scraped and scuffed the smoothed rock surface, until Arthur heard a clank behind him.

"Hans? You okay?" he asked.

Hans' armor had been caught between the rocks. He struggled and strained, but the Panzer armor was not getting through. "I'm stuck, I'm...I'm stuck!" he grunted. He swung his armored gauntlet at the walls, but they wouldn't break away.

The Sakurais slipped their way back to Hans, and Yoko struck at the rock walls with her wrist blades. Nothing seemed to help or affect them at all.

"The walls down here are much more dense than up above," Thornton noted. His glasses couldn't analyze much more than that in the dark tunnel.

"Get back, let me try something," Hans ordered. The team moved farther down the tunnel.

Walker, who was at the point, looked back at Hans with concern. "You're not going to try to—"

"I'm going to do it. Stay back," Hans boomed. He powered up the shield generators on his massive metal forearms. The view screen in his helmet lit up with warnings and alarms as he diverted power to the generators. Walker looked around as the rest of Xtremis braced themselves. Yoko and Mia huddled together away from him.

"Shut it off! You're gonna bring the whole bloody coast down on us!" Walker exclaimed as he ran, leaving the party behind.

"Hans, he's right! Stop!" Thornton shouted over the humming of the generators that were now sparking bolts of electricity. One of the bolts caught Arthur in the shoulder.

"Agh! Hans! You gotta stop!" Arthur yelled.

But Hans was focused on generating as much power as he could. *Once they get to the right power level, I can discharge the capacitors and power through this!* he thought.

"He's not listening," Mia shouted. "We have to stop him!"

Thornton threw down his trench coat, powered up one of his electrified whips and, with a crack, wrapped it around one of Hans' generators. The current jumped into Thornton's glove, and he screamed as the electricity coursed through his metallic spine. Hans immediately aborted the sequence when he saw a small explosion in his view screen.

"What happened?!" Hans waved away the smoke to see Thornton's motionless body on the ground, smoking from his now-destroyed left hand. His heart sank in his chest.

Arthur scrambled over to Thornton and sat him up. "Craig! You okay?!"

Thornton shook the cobwebs out of his head. He looked down at the destroyed gauntlet and ripped it off, the metallic mass now lifelessly attached to his spinal column. The smell of burnt hair and skin wafted through the tunnel. His hand was intact, but it was covered in second- and third-degree electrical burns.

Mia ran over to the two and began wrapping Thornton's hand in a bandage from her utility belt.

Hans looked on as tears began to well up in his eyes. The Panzer armor stood in a motionless and quiet vigil over the proceedings. "I'm sorry... Why did you do that? Why did you...?"

"Agghhh. It's okay, Hans," Thornton replied. "I'll be fine. But it looks like I'm not going to be dropping Demons with a left hook any time soon."

Hans was still motionless in his armor. "I-I can't get through. It's too– It's too tight. It's too–too closed in," he whispered.

"That's okay," Arthur said. "We're here with you. Walker's got plenty of guns. Just take the suit off, and we'll come through together."

"No, I can't... I'm not... it won't work without the suit. That's not... That's not an option.

I'm not coming out." Hans pushed back against the hole he was stuck in. "I'm sorry, I have to... I have to go." The metal of his armor groaned as he strained and pushed back against the hole.

With a screech, the armor came free. "Hans, wait!" Mia shouted.

"Go on without me. I–I am of no use to you now." With that, he retreated into the darkness of the tunnel behind the team.

The remaining members of Xtremis looked at each other in dismay as Mia helped Thornton to his feet.

Walker grimaced. "Big bratwurst is scared. I'm pretty sure he sleeps in that thing." He looked down the tunnel ahead of them. "He's not going to be any use down here, anyway."

"Hans! Get back here!" Arthur shouted into the dark tunnel behind them. With Hans gone, Thornton hurt, and Walker suspicious of his every move, Arthur knew that his allies were dwindling. He locked eyes with Mia as she finished bandaging Thornton's hand, almost as if to ask her what to do next.

Without acknowledging it, she stood up and took point.

"We still have a job to do, let's go." Mia grabbed her staff and went past Walker into the darkness. She lit the way after giving her staff a small charge. The blue hue from her staff clashed with the orange hue in the tunnel ahead of them. Walker glanced back and spat on the ground before following her in.

One by one, mankind's last hope climbed farther downward into the unknown.

CHAPTER 29

THE ENCOUNTER

Mia followed the dim light at the end of the passageway to a point where the rock walls came together. The orange glow emanated behind this particular pile of rocks that blocked their path.

"I think this is it!" she shouted back.

Arthur clambered up to the point with her, brushing past Walker whose unblinking cybernetic eyes only slightly unnerved him. He hadn't seen them that close before. He barely had time to try and forget them before he reached Mia.

"Do you think they close the path behind them once they come through?" Thornton said once he got to the point. He winced with every step, making Arthur wince sympathetically. He analyzed their current obstacle. "Walker, this is you."

"Copy that. Step back, ladies and gents." Walker set a couple of charges from his pack. He detonated them, and moments later the way was clear, giving way to an open chasm. "They probably know we're here. Keep an eye out," he warned. The cavern expanded into a deep yet bright ravine. Magma flowed through cracks in the walls, outlining the individual entries and exits into this central chamber. The heat distorted everyone's vision. A mirage of the end of the world that unfortunately was all too real.

The team climbed out onto the makeshift walkway, which wasn't so much paved as it was crunched together. Thornton noted that the walkway looked like a stream of Demon blood that had hardened into something solid. It led to a flat rock landing of rock that they could use to camp and scan the surrounding area. On the opposite side of the landing were more pathways going in different directions as well as small bridges across the magma gap.

Walker took point. He kept one of his MP5s primed, trying to keep an eye on everything around them. Mia released the charge in her staff. Considering the glowing river of magma below them, she felt they didn't need a light source anymore.

"Whatever's down here, I feel like we're getting close to it," Arthur said.

"TURN AWAY!" something said.

Arthur felt every piece of himself vibrating. Yoko brandished her wrist blades, ready for battle. Thornton, Arthur, and Walker scanned their surroundings but found nothing

Mia covered her ears. "What is that?!"

"I don't see anything," Walker shouted.

Arthur impotently grabbed the hilt of his katana. He had no idea where to swing. "IT IS NOT YOUR PLACE TO BE HERE!" the presence boomed. "BE GONE, EXTREEEMMMIIISSSS..."

Arthur and Thornton looked at each other, eyes wide with fear and confusion.

"Why does it know us? What is it?!" Walker shouted back at them, the sights of his rifle shifting and pointing all around them, trying to find the voice.

"I think it's the Demons. They know who we are and what we're doing." Thornton was trying to piece it all together.

"Sister, are you okay?" Yoko shouted in Japanese to Mia. Mia charged up her staff and recovered her balance.

"I'm fine. We have to keep moving," Mia replied. "Move!" Arthur yelled, unwittingly seconding her thought.

Their path started to crumble behind them as they made their way down. The last person across the magma gap was Arthur. He made it over with a bounding leap, embedding his grip into the cliffside to hang on. Despite his best instincts, Arthur looked down only to feel a devastating sense of vertigo. Beneath him, a ravine of flowing lava moved in between the jagged rocks.

With Thornton and Yoko's help, Arthur pulled himself up to regroup with the team. "Now what?" Walker said. "Which way do we go?"

"YOU DO NOT BELONG HERE, BRAXTON WALKERRRRR!" the presence boomed again.

Walker's cybernetic eyes went wide. "The fuck?! Come on out, you arsehole! I'll show you who belongs, you slag!" He readied his .50-cal, took a kneeling position, and eyed his surroundings.

"MIA SAKURAI, YOKO SAKURAI, YOU ARE ABOMINATIONSSSS TO NATURRRE!"

"Yoko, can you tell where it is?" Mia whispered to her sister. "I—I'm trying!" Yoko replied.

"CRAIG THORNTON, ARTHUR MORRISSS! YOU MUST DIIIIIE!" The voice echoed against the rocks.

"At least it's not insulting us, right?" Arthur quipped to Thornton, who wasn't even listening. "Yoko, I've got nothing," he said. "Can you tell where they are?"

"They... They're... all... here," she said with her eyes wide open.

The howl of the Demons enveloped the cave as every pathway lit up with the familiar glow.

"I'm really starting to hate that noise," Arthur said.

"Ready up, people!" Thornton ordered as he powered up his remaining gauntlet. The otherworldly howl grew louder as the lava-filled creatures began climbing over the edge of the cliff on all sides.

"What the hell?" Arthur said.

"Bloody—Thornton, these demons are shaped like people!" Walker shouted as he released the safety on his rifle.

"There's too many of them!" Yoko shouted. "Don't shoot!" Thornton ordered.

Walker was right. These demons were not of any of the normally recognized classifications. Gone were the Gamma and Iota classes and sizes. They had been replaced with large humanoid skeletons with fiery insides held together by the demonic transparent skin. The pit in everyone's stomachs sank.

"That's why there were no bodies!" Walker thought out loud. The missing bodies from the airfield, the wounded, even the dead, were all apparently brought here and turned into these abominations.

"Oh my god," Mia gasped as she covered her mouth.

"NO GOD YET, SWEETHEART," the presence said, less permeating than before but somehow familiar.

"Sweetheart?" Thornton tried to think. "Does that voice sound familiar to you?" he asked Arthur.

Arthur pointed his sidearm at the oncoming demons in bewilderment.

A massive thud shook the rock platform. Everyone looked to the source and grouped together in defensive stances. An enormous Demon emerged from the canyon, its glowing bright tentacles feeling around for prey.

"Walker! Kappa!" Arthur shouted.

"No... it's something else! It's bigger!" Walker studied it, trying to classify it. "You bet your ass I'm bigger," the presence said, the sound clearly coming from the monstrosity before them. "I'm larger than life, baby."

"Is that...?" Arthur looked at Thornton in disbelief. He couldn't fathom it either. "You missed me, didn't you?"

The enormous Demon revealed a human-shaped entity inside of itself, which stood up and stretched on its own. One tentacle was still attached to the back of the Demon's skull as it walked toward them.

"It's been quite the experience," it said. "I've learned so much about them. Who they are, what they do, why they're here. And why we must come together to eliminate aberrations against humanity such as yourselves."

Even without his normal skin, Thornton could tell who was walking up to them. Only one person had that much unsolicited swagger. Someone who was now their biggest threat.

"Cresher."

He gave a truly awful grin and spread his glowing arms wide. "In the Demon flesh, baby."

CHAPTER 30

IN EXTREMIS

Walker picked his jaw up off of the floor. There was no way that Cresher could have survived the crash, much less become what looked like the figurehead of this Demon invasion.

"There's no bloody way. I saw Cresher die out on the airfield!" He aimed his rifle at the Demon's head.

"Really? I recall you leaving me and Simmons to die while you played army boy." The humanoid shape gestured a finger gun at Walker, who didn't blink. "I was lucky, I turned out to be more useful than old man Simmons, after they drained everything from him."

Arthur lunged forward angrily, but Thornton held him back.

"Ooh, did I strike a nerve? I don't want to get into it, but it was disgusting what they did to him. To me, too, but I came out the other side... well, you can see." The Cresher Demon spun around and pointed at the massive shape behind him.

Thornton made a mental note of the tube that looked like it was lodged in the back of his skull. The tube was funneling the demonic liquid into Cresher's body.

"Bloody cockroach!" Walker spat.

The massive Demon unfurled five more tentacles with sharp nails at the ends. The Xtremis team backed off, readying their weapons. Arthur recognized the shape of the tentacles. *It recognized him because*

Cresher would recognize him. "This is the thing that attacked the ship!" he shouted. "It was Cresher!"

"That's how they knew where it was," Mia confirmed. Her staff was at full charge. Yoko brandished her wrist blades as she woozily shook her head. The presence of this new Alpha Demon was wreaking havoc on her psychic abilities.

"That's right, baby doll! And once you all join the right side of this war, you will all see the truth. Then, like me, you shall truly be free!" Cresher pointed at the team, and the five tentacles shot towards each of them.

Arthur dodged his and swiped at it with his katana. The metal clanged off the sharp, rocky tip as it whipped around to get at him. "I assume you are all familiar with the slash and burn farming technique?" Cresher continued as the team fought for their lives. "Of course you do, what am I saying? You're all mega super geniuses. So for the ACTOR in the room, I'll explain..."

Mia swung her staff, which clanged off of the tentacle aimed at her head. She ducked under its next attempt, which barely missed her hairline. She raised her staff up and supported the weight of her sister, who jumped up and slashed the one chasing her in a brilliant and brutal display. Yoko's tentacle shrieked and spouted its Demon blood everywhere, singeing Yoko's armor.

"When farmers don't have anywhere left to plant their crops, they burn and cut down parts of the forest to make room for more crops..."

Arthur swung his katana wildly, but his attacker dodged and swiped right back at him. The glowing arm wrapped around his legs and the arm holding his sword.

"Since mankind has decided to completely burn everything down and use all the planet's resources we are here to... Oh, he's not even listening." The Cresher Demon lamented.

Arthur fell to the ground, trying to hold the tentacle back. The tentacle squeezed and wriggled around him, trying to get through his hands. He slipped one hand to his leg holster and snagged his Desert Eagle. Two successive blasts, and the tentacle fell limp all around his body.

Catching his breath, Arthur said to himself, "I've been on the internet long enough to know where that was going to go..." He looked over at the team. Mia had somehow gotten separated from the group and was fighting her attacker by herself near the rock ledge. "Hold on, Mia!" he shouted as he dashed towards her.

Thornton activated his remaining whip and cracked it, attempting to get a hold of the tentacle attacking him. Almost as if he were the aggressor, he ducked and lunged. He kept his boxing stance and finally wrapped his whip around the tentacle. He delivered an electric charge to the enormous beast, making it howl in pain.

Thornton wrapped the tentacle around his gauntlet until he had the tip in his grasp. "Walker!" he shouted.

Walker dove under the tentacle, rolled to Thornton, and pulled the trigger on his shotgun. As the two shielded their eyes, the tentacle exploded, with a splash of magma spewing from its tip. Walker's own attacker shot towards him only to be met with a blast from the other sawed-off shotgun. Walker threw off his duster coat, which had caught fire. The numerous holsters and weapons he kept close to his body were visible as he grabbed the two MP5s hanging from his side.

Mia swung her staff, clanging it off of the sharp talon. Her feet were edging closer to the cliffside, and she nearly lost her balance. The tentacle made one final dive at her face, but Mia put up her staff to protect herself. Instead of trying to penetrate her defense the tentacle wrapped around her staff, yanked it out of her hands, and flung it to the far side of the cliff.

Mia was disarmed. Alone on the cliff, she kept her eye on the attacking tentacle. Perhaps she could defeat this monster with her hands, she thought, as she prepared for a final strike.

In a blur she was pushed to the ground away from the edge. She hit her head and was in a daze, she couldn't tell what happened. Yoko rushed over to her side and helped her up.

"You okay?"

"What happened?"

"It's... look."

Yoko pointed over to a metal shape that Mia finally made out to be Arthur. But something was wrong. Her attacker has lodged itself into Arthur's mouth. The sounds of his chokes echoed off of the chamber walls.

"ARTHUR!" Thornton shouted.

"Get back!" Walker barked at the Sakurai sisters. Yoko pulled Mia away from Arthur as she fought to reach him to try and help.

"Ah, yessssss. The golden boy. Of all the potential in this chamber, you were the most valuable. Welcome to the other side," the Cresher Demon spoke. Thornton assumed Cresher would be smiling if he had real lips. Arthur gagged as something was happening to him from inside.

"It's trying to turn him!"

Yoko leapt and slashed the tentacle. The Alpha Demon howled in pain and retracted all of its deflated tentacles. Arthur yanked the talon out of his throat and coughed up blood and hot magma. Yoko took a defensive stance in front of Arthur, making sure no more tentacles came their way.

Arthur screamed in pain; it was worse than the day he woke up, searing the back of his throat with a sharp piercing he could feel at the bottom of his skull. Blood clogged his airway, until everything stopped all at once. Arthur fell silent and dropped his hands, his left still clutching his sword.

"The transfer is complete. We no longer require any of you. Do we, Arthur?" Cresher addressed the group as the Alpha Demon behind him raised up on its two remaining legs.

Mia slid over to where her staff had landed. She grabbed it, removing her gloves and began recharging. Yoko glanced behind her at Arthur who stood there, unmoving, looking down with his hair covering his face.

"What is it, Arthur?" Yoko asked. "I can see now," he said quietly.

"Shit." Yoko spun and swung her wrist blade at his neck.

Without looking, Arthur blocked and held her attack with his katana blade. He slowly raised his head, the look in his eyes burning with madness.

"Mankind needs to be destroyed," he uttered through clenched teeth.

Yoko's eyes went wide. She lifted her opposite hand to strike but was immediately struck in the chest and launched back at the group, landing in a heap before them. Walker trained his weapons at Arthur's head as Thornton checked on her. Arthur activated his face shield and held his katana with both hands, steady and solid.

"Good, I have no more use for the rest of them. You may dispose of them as you wish. Or feast, I don't care. I'm not your mother," Cresher commanded the silent, unmoving, humanoid Demons surrounding the area.

With a supernatural howl the Demons began advancing on the group. Walker fired round after round into the oncoming horde, dropping them with headshots one by one. Their heads popped with a sickly crunch as magma spilled onto the pathway below.

Thornton shook Yoko to try and bring her back to her feet, but Arthur ran directly at them with katana drawn, ready to strike. Yoko saw him coming. From her supine position, she flicked on her flame-thrower and blew a massive plume of fire directly at him.

Arthur held back and covered up, avoiding any damage.

Yoko shut her thrower off and threw herself out of Thornton's grip and towards Arthur. She came down overhead with a slashing strike that Arthur blocked with minimal effort. Yoko spun around with her other wrist blade, which was batted away.

Thornton slid over to Walker's side. He took the MP5 that was hanging off of his free shoulder and opened fire on the demon horde. Walker slapped in his last clip as the batch of humanoid Demons edged closer and closer.

"Seventeen. Eighteen. Nineteen," Walker counted his headshots. Thornton's grip was compromised by his injured hand, but he did his best to make sure nothing else got close.

The metal from Arthur's katana clanged with Yoko's wrist blades.

"Wake up, asshole. I can't believe we have to do this now," she uttered to herself in Japanese as she ducked one of Arthur's swipes.

"The only thing you have to do is die!" Arthur responded, remarkably in perfect Japanese.

Bewildered, Yoko barely managed to catch his sword with her wrist blades right in front of her face.

"That's right, our boy here is programmed for so much more than you know. And seeing as he is more machine than man, he can be repurposed. There's barely anything human about him left anyway. I don't even understand why they chose him as humanity's savior... He –AGH!"

Cresher's boasting was cut short. Mia had cracked him in the face with her staff, and the Demon dropped to the floor. She had lifted her staff and was trying to slam it down onto Cresher's head when she was shoved to the ground.

Arthur stood over her, brimming with rage. He grasped the hilt of his katana and spun it around to stab downward into Mia's heart. His thrust was batted away with a clang from Yoko as she dove behind him to get a closer attack position. Mia spun up to her feet, and the two sisters stood on opposite sides of Arthur.

"You don't have to do this, Arthur!" Mia shouted over the pops of the gunfire behind them. Arthur twitched for a split second before grabbing the hilt of his sword and splitting it in two, his stance locked between the two women. Yoko swung first, and Mia spun her staff, trying to keep him off-balance. The three augmented humans battled in a flurry of strikes and slashes. Thrusts and parries clashed between their weapons. Mia ducked under a swipe with Arthur's left hand and blocked a follow-up attack with his right. He turned around with a kick to her sternum and leapt back towards Yoko, bringing both weapons down on her head. Yoko managed to catch them by crossing her blades together and pushing back. The two held in their clash as Arthur tried to force his blades through hers. The edge of his katana started cutting into her hands as she gave way. She yelped in pain as she strained to hold him off.

Walker turned for a moment and fired a single shot at Arthur's head. Almost instantaneously, Arthur turned around and swung his katana to deflect the bullet. With his free hand he punched Yoko in the jaw, putting her down on the ground. He stepped menacingly toward Walker who opened fire. Arthur deflected any bullets that were aimed directly at any vitals, and his armor deflected the rest.

"Eh, cripes," Walker muttered as he dropped his MP5 and slipped out a bowie knife. "Walker! Damn it!" Thornton shouted as he ran out of ammo. Powering up his gauntlet, he slammed the metal fist onto a walk-way the Demons were using to get to their plateau. It crumbled and fell into the rock quarry below them, taking several of the creatures with it.

Walker flipped his knife to the tip and threw it. Arthur dropped his katana, caught it, and flung it back him. The knife lodged itself into Walker's thigh just above the knee. Walker grunted and fell down, clutching his leg.

Yoko held her jaw as she shouted to Mia, "There's something inside him! I felt it! Get it out of him! It's getting bigger!"

Thornton slid over to another bridge and slammed his gauntlet down. This one was sturdier than the last. He slammed it a few more times, not noticing Arthur stalking him, moving closer to him. Arthur raised his sword, aimed it directly at the back of Thornton's neck. Thornton's glasses triggered a proximity warning and flashed in his eyes. He slipped out and blocked the attack with his active gauntlet. Thornton swung with his electrified whip but Arthur slipped, ducked, and jumped around the whipcracks.

Arthur spun and caught the gauntlet under his arm. He leaned in close to Thornton and whispered with a look of madness in his eye, "Not today, young man." He flipped Thornton over his head to the ground. Thornton's glasses flew to the side as Arthur stomped on the gauntlet, destroying it along with his wrist inside. Thornton screamed in agony.

Walker had not given up yet. He pulled out two pistols and fired at Arthur who stood, unmoving, on Thornton's arm. The bullets were completely ineffective. Walker tried dragging himself closer to them and fired a couple of headshots at some Demons that were edging closer to them.

Arthur looked down on Thornton who was meekly trying to push him off of the wreckage that was once his gauntlet. With the power cut off, the whip lay lifeless around him. Thornton looked up at Arthur, his eyes welling up from the pain and the struggle to break free. Arthur reached down and pulled the overdrive trigger out of the remains of Thornton's gauntlet. He looked at it for a moment before he swapped it with his Desert Eagle from his leg holster. He aimed it directly at Thornton's head. The pull of the trigger, though, was met with a soft click.

He was out of ammo.

Suddenly, a block of ice threw Arthur clear and to the ground. Mia formed another chunk of ice with her staff and heaved it at him. Arthur got to his feet and smashed through this block of ice and another.

Mia spun her staff and pointed it at him, the light on the tip of her staff shining as bright as ever. She cooled the air in front of her as fast as she could, concentrating on the area between her and Arthur. If she could just freeze him in place, then they can deal with this looming demonic threat. The fog of the rapidly cooling air surrounded Arthur, forcing him back even as he tried to push through it all. The gusts of cold air were forcing him to clamp into the ground. Slowly, he reached for the overdrive trigger that he had taken from Thornton.

Mia saw that he was reaching back and redoubled her efforts to freeze him in place. This was her only chance to stop Arthur from killing them all. He strained to hold onto the trigger and slowly lifted his thumb up. He tried to push through the cold freezing all of his joints, but he could go no further. He completely froze in place.

Mia collapsed in a heap, drained from her effort. She looked up just in time to catch Arthur's hand breaking through the ice and pushing the trigger.

CHAPTER 31

EX INFERIS

The Cresher Demon grabbed Mia by the throat. "It was a good effort, really. But now, mankind's greatest triumph will be its downfall!"
Mia gasped for air and kicked at Cresher to no effect.

Arthur's frozen body shuddered and cracked through the ice until he burst free with a powerful scream. Ice shards flew in every direction, forcing the team to cover up. The overdrive trigger was engaged and had removed all the limits Thornton and Simmons had on Arthur, finally freeing him to his full potential.

"Witness the fall of man!" Cresher bellowed. Arthur's primal scream reverberated off of the cavernous walls. The Demons stopped their attack and watched as Arthur's body glowed with searing hot metal as he convulsed from head to toe.

Then as quickly as it all began, something inside Arthur snapped. Smoke billowed out of his mouth and various points in his body. He slumped to one knee.

"What's happening?" The Cresher Demon threw Mia to the ground. "You useless tin can! I told Simmons this is what you get when he's more metal than flesh! Destroy them all!"

Arthur sighed with relief. "Phew, that's..." He interrupted himself by vomiting up a piece of rock, the parasite that had been lodged in his throat. The rock cracked against the rock floor covered in bile and blood.

He shook his head, getting reoriented. "The hell? What happened?"

"You almost killed us," Yoko said as she drove her blades into the jaw of the Demon next to her. "That thing that was inside of you, I can't feel it anymore."

"The parasite is out. Arthur, your limits are off! We can end this now!" Thornton yelled. Arthur stood up and looked at his hands. The heads-up display in his eyes lit up green.

"You're right, I understand now. I understand everything. The overdrive was going to melt my brain, but it diverted to the parasite."

Limiters removed

Efficiency at 100%

Threat level Alpha

Objective: Stop Demon advancement

Current Target: Former Peter Cresher/Alpha Demon

Arthur ran at full speed at the Cresher Demon and, in a flash, gave him a right hook to the jaw and a knee to the gut. He grabbed the back of his neck and yanked out the tube connecting him with the massive demon near him.

"No!" Cresher shouted. He tried to hold the back of his head to prevent any more fluid from spewing out. He fell to the ground in a heap. The massive Alpha Demon roared in pain as did every other Demon in the caves. The ungodly sound reverberated through the Xtremis team's bones. Arthur stepped away from the Alpha Demon, and slid back to Mia who was bruised on her neck from Cresher's claws.

"Are you all right?" he asked her. His voice was bolder, more confident. Mia coughed. "I'm fine. But we have to... keep fighting."

"You wait here. I've got this," Arthur said. He stood and squared up defiantly to the Alpha Demon that was still flailing in pain.

The Demon fell silent as it noticed Arthur standing before it. It rose up to its full height, several stories tall. Arthur craned his neck up to try and stay eye to eye with the monster. He swallowed hard.

The Alpha Demon roared with unholy rage as it swung its giant fists down at Arthur who leapt out of the way and bounded to his feet. The impact shook the platform, and Thornton noticed it starting to lower into the magma. "We gotta get out of here!"

Yoko helped Thornton to his feet as he threw off his mangled gauntlet. She grimaced as Thornton popped his wrist back into place with a scream.

Arthur bounced and flipped around the Alpha's swipes, barely missing the massive arms.

Missing: Primary Weapon

Secondary Weapon Ammo: Empty

Locating...

Found

"Mia! My swor—OOF." Arthur was swatted aside like a fly by the huge Demon's claw. He tumbled to the ground and nearly fell off of their sinking platform.

The Alpha Demon turned its attention to the rest of the group. It raised a craggy claw up high to slam down on them. Mia held her staff up at full charge and slammed it down, creating a protective barrier around them all. The Demon brought its tentacle down but stopped before it collided with the icy dome. Mia looked behind her. Yoko had her hands up, trying to hold the gigantic demon in place with her mental ability. Her body quivered as she gave everything she had to hold this beast back.

"Yoko!"

"I. Can't. Keep—" Yoko spat blood as it drained out of her nose into her mouth.

The Alpha Demon struggled to push down, but its arm was stuck in place. It shook violently as it tried to crush them all. The Demon roared as it strained against her power.

"Hold on!" Mia shouted. She could see Arthur's katana on the ground just outside of the dome.

Yoko was starting to fade. She collapsed into Walker's arms as the Demon's fist slammed into the dome, shattering the ice and sending the team flying. Walker tried his best to cover Yoko and protect her from the ice shards falling around them.

Arthur held on to the edge of the cliff with all of his strength. Using his momentum, he swung back to the top, sprinted towards the Alpha Demon, and leapt onto its arm. The Demon flailed in an attempt to shake Arthur off.

BOOM.

The Alpha Demon screeched in pain. BOOM.

BOOM!

The arm that Arthur was clinging to flew off and writhed until it cooled into a rock formation. Arthur bounded and landed on his feet. The Alpha Demon howled. He looked back and smiled at the readout. He never thought he would be this happy to see him.

"HANS!"

CHAPTER 32

REDEEMER

Hans Schreiber, missing the upper portion of his armor, held his modified rail gun in his massive grip. Flanking him were the SEALS led by Joshua and McGahee. They fanned out and fired on the Demons. The rail gun smoked as Hans powered it up for another shot on the Alpha Demon.

"Last shot, my friend!" he shouted to Arthur. Arthur looked to Walker who held his katana.

He nodded.

The final shot from the rail gun blasted the left leg out from underneath the Alpha Demon, bringing it down to one stump, screaming. Arthur leapt into the air high above the monstrosity. Walker threw the sword at Arthur as hard as he could. Arthur adjusted in midair to catch it.

"Damn," Walker uttered.

"What? It was a good throw," Thornton said. "I was aiming for his head."

Arthur pushed every bit of his energy into his blade. He came down with it through the entirety of the beast and landed in a crouch in front of it. The Alpha Demon stopped screeching and stood there, almost puzzled. Arthur calmly stood up, returned his katana to its sheath on his back, and faced the group.

"The hell?" Walker asked.

The Alpha Demon roared and split down its middle as an eruption of lava spewed forth.

Arthur sped over to the backside of the group and kicked a few approaching humanoid Demons off of the cliff's edge.

"We have to go. This place is falling apart," he calmly said.

"Covering fire!" Joshua shouted. The SEALs began lighting up the cavern with gunfire. Hans ran down the pathway to the group and picked up Yoko. Mia helped Thornton and Walker towards safety. Arthur spun and ducked, moving from enemy to enemy, slicing them to ribbons, performing a dance of death the likes of which no one had seen or expected out of him. Once the pathway was clear he sheathed his katana and moved towards the group. At the cavern exit, he turned and looked back at the Cresher Demon's corpse. Except... it was still glowing with the light of his blood.

Arthur checked his readings.

Scanning...

Target: Former Peter Cresher

Status: Alive

Arthur was stunned. He made his way back to Cresher's body on the ground. Cresher was unresponsive but writhing in pain. The back of his head had solidified where the tube had been ripped out.

"You really are a cockroach, aren't you?" Arthur raised his boot to stomp him out, but something made him hesitate. Slowly, Arthur put his boot back down and sighed to himself. "Walker is going to hate me even more than he already does. Come on." He reached down and pulled Cresher up onto his shoulders in a fireman's carry and calmly followed the group out of the cave.

Cresher coughed up some fluid before sputtering out, "Why?"

"I honestly don't know. If you know what's best for you, you'll keep pretending to be dead."

The SEALs moved in two-by-two formation back through the caverns. McGahee helped Yoko through, and Joshua helped Hans carry Walker and Thornton back to the evac point. Eventually they came to the entrance ravine where the Fulton packs awaited them. The SEALs reattached to their carabiners and began their ascent back up the rock wall. McGahee and Mia helped Yoko strap on her Fulton pack. Before pulling the cord, Mia gave her sister a tight hug.

"We did it, let's get you home safe."

Yoko could only let out a meager, "Good."

Mia pulled the cord, and the balloon instantly filled and pulled Yoko up and out of the cave. "Don't worry, ma'am. We'll take good care of her," McGahee reassured Mia before heading up the rock wall. Mia watched as her sister was lifted out, and managed to give her a salute before she went out of sight. She sighed in relief for a brief moment before completely freezing in her tracks. Thornton stopped Joshua from helping him with his pack and turned to look at the bright orange glow coming down the pathway.

"Bloody hell." Walker drew a huge revolver from his waistband and aimed it down the pathway. He limped to a covered position on the outside of the entryway. The glow stepped into view, and Walker fired. The .50-caliber shell ricocheted off of the cavern wall as Arthur stepped back out of the way.

"Hold your fire! It's me!" he shouted.

"That means nothing to me!" Walker popped off three more rounds. "Whoa! What are you on about?" Thornton shouted at Walker. "Dammit." Arthur cursed to himself as he dropped Cresher's limp body.

"What are you doing with him?! He should have been buried with the rest of them back there!" Walker yelled.

"He's still alive. We can use him."

"Are you sure?" Walker demanded. "Are you sure he's not using you? How do I know you're not still under their control?" He kept his aim steady as he leaned against the entryway, his weapon still pointed down the tunnel.

"I'm telling you, I'm fine now. We can talk this over!" Arthur shouted. "Walker, that's enough! Lower your weapon," Thornton ordered.

"Fuck off, Thornton! He might be your pet project, but he's a fuckin' danger to me, you, her, and every human still alive out there!" Walker fired off one more shot.

"*Scheisse!*" Hans winced. "Walker please!" He wanted to get out of that tunnel faster than everyone else. He felt exposed as he glanced up the crevasse. This tense situation wasn't helping his anxiety in the slightest.

"I know it's scary. It's terrifying even for me. But you gotta trust me here. We can find out what they did to him and Simmons an—"

"Simmons?!" Walker yelped. His voice almost cracked, "You don't know if Cresher gave him up or fed him to the demons himself!"

"And that's what we're going to find out! He's going to be my responsibility!"

"I'd rather not deal with either one of you if I had my way, to be perfectly fair."

"Well this is all you've got! Me! And I don't think I can do this without any of you." Arthur surprised himself when he said it. "Like it or not, we're in this together!"

Walker checked his rifle's sight. "You're right. I don't like it. In fact, I'm really fuckin' pissed I'm even a part of this. If you bring that thing back, I'm out!"

"Walker! Stand down!" Thornton stepped up as Mia held him back. He gave her a surprised look. She looked back with her icy blue eyes that felt heavy and sorrowful. The dried blood from everyone's injuries stained her armor. She felt tired and beaten, and wanted it all to be over.

"Trust your teammates, Craig," she said to him.

"He'll kill us all! Right, Thornton?! Your words!" Walker shouted. Thornton could only look at the ground.

"I'm coming out!" Arthur took a breath. He grabbed Cresher's arm and dragged his Demon form behind him. He stuck his hand out and slowly leaned around the corner. Walker still had his revolver trained on him. Arthur made sure his body was between Walker and Cresher.

"Bloody tin can," Walker spat.

"I'm sorry about your leg. I'm sorry about the demons, the planet, all of it. But he might be the key to beating them once and for all. If you can just trust me, I will show you," Arthur pleaded.

"I can't just trust you!" Walker bellowed. "Them? Them I trust! Because they're flesh and blood, like me!" He gestured toward the rest of the team. "But you? I saw the look in your eyes. They weren't human. You are a robot, completely reprogrammable, and lacking a soul. You aren't one of us."

"I..." Arthur had a moment to himself. "I honestly don't know much about what I am."

"And that's the scary part. Even if I pulled this trigger, I have no guarantee it'll actually do anything to you." Walker slowly lowered his weapon. His eyes dropped to the floor, hanging in shame. "I can't go through and complete this mission if I have to watch my back to make sure you aren't stabbing it."

"I promise that isn't going to happen."

"He's my responsibility, Walker," Thornton said.

"None of your words mean dick to me." Walker dropped his weapon. "I'm out."

Mia, Hans, and Thornton all slumped when they heard it. Arthur tried to say something, anything, but the words wouldn't come to him. He didn't have any clue how to stop him. Walker limped past the rest of the team and yanked his Fulton pack from Joshua.

"If you lot want to stay alive yourselves, you'll do the same thing." With that, he pulled the cord and left the cave, and Xtremis, behind.

SAN ANDREAS

Six months later...

Somewhere near the Demonic Territory Border

The IAV Stryker V2 rumbled over the dusty terrain. In the distance, the howls of the demons warned of oncoming obstacles in the mission ahead. Hans Schreiber a.k.a. Panzer was flying overhead, scanning the area.

"Everything is clear for the next two klicks. I shall meet you there after I secure the landing zone. Panzer out." Hans fired off his jets and sped on ahead of the slower transport.

Inside the transport, the Xtremis team gathered together as they rocked back and forth over the bumpy terrain.

"Okay, you heard the man. It's almost showtime!" Arthur a.k.a. Swift Eagle dusted off his jacket and glanced at the Xtremis logo on his shoulder before checking the magazine in his Desert Eagle. It was a raised circular X that had an American flag pattern. He still wasn't comfortable with the branding but knew it was best to keep getting support for the team.

Everyone was ever so slightly more marketable. Shiny upgrades to all of their equipment, each etched with the XTREMIS name in tiny letters. Some of the team took to it better than others. Hans was fine as long as nobody touched his armor but himself. The new guys were fine with it. Arthur still had his reservations about all the marketing. He felt like he was being kitted out like an action figure to sell to kids. But ultimately if it got them more funding and more personnel then he was fine with it.

"Everyone knows the plan, so I'm not going to depress you by getting into it. I will say that I'm proud of what this team has done to prepare for our mission today. Joshua!"

"Sir!" Joshua a.k.a. Bloodshot replied. No longer a SEAL but a full-fledged member of the team, Joshua had assumed Walker's role as sharpshooter in his absence. His AWES equipment had seen some scuffs and repairs over his time on the team. He swapped the standard issue military helmet to an armored mask that private military companies liked to use. It was black all around except the eyes which were painted white with red trim. On the edge written in bold letters was the word **BLOODSHOT**. Arthur kept telling him how cool that name was and how he needs to trademark that as soon as possible.

"I don't expect anything crazy. Just keep them off our flanks, and it'll be a good day. We will get you back home to your wife, Angel, in time for dinner!"

"You got it, boss! Can we push this 'till after dinner? My wife's cooking is terrible!" He laughed.

"Thornton, do you read me? Come in, Bolt Fist!" Arthur pulled up a call on the HUD in his helmet.

"Reading you, old man. How are you feeling?" Thornton a.k.a. Bolt Fist answered from the forward operating base. He was the only one who didn't care for his codename.

"Good go to, young man. The cockroach giving you any issues?"

"I'll have you know that the only reason any of this is happening is because I gave the original say-so," a voice on the line spoke up.

Thornton smirked and looked over to the person next to him. Cresher, still in his demonic form but now wearing the snazziest business suit he could fit into, grabbed the microphone. "So don't go thinking you can call me names. I have a name, I—"

Thornton took the radio back.

"He's fine, he's just grumpy he can't wear his shoes like he used to."

"Make him some Heelys, he'll like that. This mission goes well, we'll never have to listen to him again." He glanced over at Mia. "How is Yoko doing?"

"She's making progress, but she's not ready for the field just yet." Arthur could hear Yoko a.k.a. Brimstone swearing at them in Japanese. Thornton answered, "She sends her love to quote 'Mia and only Mia,' so that's everybody. McGahee says she will be mission ready in no time.."

"Thanks, man. I'll check in at the designated times. You know, unless I'm dead and all." Arthur gave a two-finger tap on the headset to Thornton before signing off.

On the other side of the transport, Mia a.k.a. Ice Angel sat checking her staff for any abnormalities. Everything seemed to be working well. Arthur looked over to her. When her eyes met his, all he could muster was a nod. She gave him a smirk, and, as she was wearing her sister's wrist blades, she began sharpening them.

"I have a good feeling about this!" Tommy a.k.a. Black Fuse said. The Ireland and Greenland territories decided he would be of use to the team and had sent him over as soon as they heard Xtremis was recruiting. Tommy smiled as he took one last look at his bag of explosives jostling around in the back of the transport.

"God, I love your optimism! As terrifying as that is, try not to blow us up yet!" Arthur smiled. Tommy gave him a big thumbs-up with an almost demented smile on his face.

Arthur sat back and steeled himself for the mission. These new recruits would be a huge boost to the credibility of the program. The Irish munitions expert, two former Navy SEALs, whoever this Russian liaison was going to be. As long as they survived the day, everything else would be like clockwork. For the first time in a long time, Arthur felt optimistic about the future. Maybe they could pull this off.

The buzzer went off, and the red light clicked on. Arthur gave the signal. They were prepared for this. They were ready. The new Xtremis team popped open the latch and moved out into the desert sun.

JOSE DEGRACIA IS an Author, Actor, Professional Wrestler, and Owner of an arcade bar in his home town of Jacksonville, Florida. A Navy veteran, Jose has his hands in every aspect of entertainment. With a Bachelor's degree in Film, he spends his time hosting events, serving drinks at his bar, Rec Room, acting on stage or on screen, creating short films, writing screen plays, or training to get to the next level of professional wrestling at Dvon Dudley Academy in Orlando, Florida.

His short film he wrote and directed, Family Virtues, has been selected and screened both at the Orlando Film Festival and internationally at the Cannes International Film Festival.

He can often be found on the independent wrestling scene in the southeast United States in and around Florida, Georgia, and the Carolinas wrestling as The Karibbean Kid.

CPSIA information can be obtained
at www.ICGtesting.com
Printed in the USA
BVHW041040240921
617462BV00008B/722/J

9 781737 338307